THE GREEN PLATOON

Dedication

Etc.,

Etc.,

Erin, Taylor, Carl

For the Counsellor,

Noeleen

Is Fionn O'Toole a soldier or a saviour?

THE GREEN PLATOON

MARTIN HAND

ETC Publishing

First published in 2020 by ETC Publishing
Dublin
Ireland
https://www.facebook.com/martin.hand.733
martinhand767@gmail.com

Amazon paperback	ISBN: 978 1 78846 158 0
Paperback	ISBN: 978 1 78846 155 9
eBook – mobi format	ISBN: 978 1 78846 156 6
eBook – ePub format	ISBN: 978 1 78846 157 3

Produced by Kazoo Independent Publishing Services
222 Beech Park, Lucan, Co. Dublin
www.kazoopublishing.com

Kazoo Independent Publishing Services is not the publisher of this work. All rights and responsibilities pertaining to this work remain with ETC Publishing.

Cover design by Andrew Brown

Printed in the EU

Chapter **One**

Christmas spirit in the middle of Halloween was 'all my arse' according to Joe, who was explaining his reasoning to his buddy Fionn. He went further: 'You see, Fionn, all this Catholic stuff from the commandant is a leftover from the days when the Church added to an illusion – the illusion that it contributed to the backbone of command and leadership.'

On hearing no reply, Joe went on: 'Ordering us to attend an early Christmas Mass on the first of November … I mean, come on now.'

'Fall on your knees/ O hear the angels' voices,' rang out in the chapel, drowning out Joe's mumblings.

Commandant O'Mahony was a leftover from the time when a good Catholic ethos was at the heart of the Irish Army establishment. The British military had tradition; the Irish had religion. So an early Christmas Mass was just the ticket, and mandatory, no less – an order.

'O night divine/ O night when Christ was born.'

'Jesus, that blonde one can hold a note, can't she?' Joe said.

Still not a peep out of Fionn. Joe wasn't getting irked though. It was still sinking in, the happening, the event in Wicklow last week. It had been the last week of basic training, and it would leave a memory that wouldn't fade. Not ever.

Soon the boys would be close enough to the Holy Land, albeit in the less fashionable Lebanon. UN peacekeeping, the Irish. Jesus, that was an anomaly if ever there was one. In fairness the boys in green were good at it, and a few of them had made the ultimate sacrifice. Dead, in other words. Blessed are the peacemakers, but how did the Irish get away with it? The bloody fighting Irish, drink-induced fighting, usually.

But when it came to foreigners, the Irish did have something. None of the enlisted men would look a Lebanese or Syrian in the eye and think, *I'm better than you.* That wasn't a magical gift, more a freak of geography. This peripheral island on the edge of Europe would instil in you the sense that you're small, insignificant, and that the only way is up. No need to be looking down on some poor bastard who had even less than you. Fionn and Joe, two soldiers from Dublin, had no delusions of grandeur.

Mass ground on. Joe didn't know why, but whenever he saw choirs on the television they were always made up of old fellas and youngish women. The choir he saw before him was no exception.

'Joy to the world/ the Lord has come.'

The lads appreciated one break with tradition. The women had broken into the citadel. The choir from Holy Faith Cabra had been recruited. Commandant

O'Mahony probably told an underling to start with Christ Church or Saint Patrick's and work his way down. You must have standards, and there was no way Christ Church's choir would be singing carols in early November on the northside of Dublin.

The edifice of McKee Barracks on Blackhorse Ave, unaffectionately known as the Tsar's Winter Palace, certainly benefited from the presence of a bit of female glamour, at least from the young soldiers' point of view. Perhaps the girls didn't look like they would make the cover of *Vogue* anytime soon, but still the boys were well pleased to see them. *A bit of flesh – no harm on a black Saturday evening*, Joe thought, while Fionn maintained his silence. Seven days until departure, and a once-off pass for the officers' mess. Drinks and finger food after Mass. At least it was something to look forward to.

The platoon, including Joe and Fionn, sat together on the right-hand side of the barracks chapel, with the parents and the girlfriends of those who had them on the left. It was like an awkward wedding. Mary and Dermot, Joe's ma and da, were there, as was Fionn's mother, Margaret. There was no da, never had been.

There was a dynamic between Mary and Margaret. Mary was competitive, Margaret wasn't. This was not the sole basis for their friendship, but it had at least laid a solid foundation for it. The other thing they had in common was that they had one child, a son, each. The two boys had grown up like brothers, which was a good thing because it choked the potential for selfishness out of the two only children.

The platoon was a mix of three mid-thirties career soldiers and the eight kids, eighteen to twenty-two-year-olds, the new recruits. The conversation between Joe's parents, at the passing-out parade, centred on Dermot's fears that mid-thirties men and spotty youngsters were usually a recipe for bullying. He remembered the primary-school days of forty years previously. Bullies in abundance.

Fionn's mother expressed a different view. 'Sure wouldn't the older men look after the youngsters, show them the ropes and that?' You never knew with Margaret if the force of her Christian spirit was winning in its battle over the corporeal world. Margaret was different, funny, but she was no eejit. Dermot wouldn't put up with an eejit as a friend, in any case.

Dermot Brennan had grown up in the Finglas of the late seventies, where, by his own assessment, bullies in school outnumbered the decent guys by a ratio of two to one. A slight exaggeration, perhaps. Dermot was one of those quintessential Dubliners that everybody knows at least one example of, the type given to the belief that a bird might be known for its song but a man should be known for his conversation. Dermot liked to quote Brendan Behan-type phrases. For example, 'The dead arose and appeared to many,' might be a dig at Joe if he had slept late. But he was an intelligent and decent man nonetheless. He had come up the hard way and was the better for it, he thought. In childhood, he was too meek to deal with those schoolyard hard chaws. In adulthood he had become opinionated. He was better and had done better than them. There were a lot of gobshites about, and no better man than Dermot to bring this fact to their attention.

Margaret was a pleasant-looking woman with zero sex appeal. The platoon youngsters wouldn't be sledging Fionn over his yummy mummy. The same might not be true for Joe, however. His ma, Mary, was a looker in her mid-forties. Dermot was always mildly put out that it was his wife who attracted male attention over single Margaret when the three of them were out for the night. The world didn't run according to Dermot's parallel lines. If it did, Margaret would have given in to Mary's teasing and got into this swipe right, swipe left thing. Things of the world of social media.

'The work of the Devil,' Margaret would call it in reply. She was recalling a phrase used by her own mother, years back, and not necessarily expressing her own piety.

The comb-over tenor boomed out, 'Jerusalem, Jerusalem' – not really a Christmas song but given where the boys were heading, it was kind of appropriate. To most of the platoon, the location of Jerusalem was a bit unclear. All they knew for certain was that the Lebanon was a four-and-a-half-hour flight away, somewhere deserty.

When the Mass was finally over, it was time for the

lads to test their charms with the choir's wans. The congregation made their way across the marching square. The smell of the previous day's bonfires still hung in the air. The girls made themselves scarce, probably to touch up their make-up. Fair play to them for finding a private nook in an army barracks. But the female spirit can be indomitable when the game is afoot.

The lads were more interested in getting the first pint down in time to relax their own vocal cords. The curmudgeon Jimmy O'Rourke was behind his bar. What Jimmy understood about customer service could be written on the back of a stamp. O'Rourke was a civilian who would never have lasted in a public bar. In the officers' mess, he was the commandant and he got away with dishing out insulting remarks from rank to rank. This suited his cantankerous nature.

Jimmy had maintained a bullying scowl all day. His bar was busy with privates, so many of them that he wouldn't have the time, or the wit, to dish out insults to the young soldiers. He hadn't had the sense to call in reinforcements to man the bar for the couple of hours that it would be busy. Instead in his head he would serve the civilians first, then the two sergeants and then the enlisted men.

Dermot managed to get his pint ordered and two of those small bottles of red wine for Mary and Margaret. He had started a conversation with O'Rourke about procuring a full bottle of red, value for money and all that.

'This is an officers' mess, my good man,' O'Rourke scowled back, setting the tone for the hell he expected would exist for the next few hours. He rabbited on, to the point that his customers were given to choose the hard stuff, nonchalantly pointing behind him to the whiskey and brandy dispensers as he finished off the head of Dermot's pint. He was making a point to the separate queues of sergeants and privates – or 'grunts', as Jimmy referred to them – that were forming at the bar. Jimmy was not to be rushed, not without a miracle anyway.

The girls arrived a little while after the initial melee at the bar. A ripple of excitement permeated the room. They looked good as they discreetly surveyed the mess to see where they should set up camp. The comb-overs had established themselves at a large bench near the fire, leaving room that they hoped would be filled by the girls. The single soldiers had made the strategic mistake of ganging together at the right end of the bar. This would have been a good ploy in a theatre of war but not so good on the battlefield of flirtation.

Margaret and Mary did their own clandestine surveying of the girls. A mother's prerogative. Mary was observing a blonde who was wearing a tight black dress and matching tights. There was a dawning realisation that her boy was in competition and where he finished in the field was a reflection on her.

Margaret was a different fish. The normal ways of

the world did not fit with her.

'Would you let your daughter out like that blonde one over there?' Mary asked.

'Mary, that's a twenty-ish-year-old woman. You were married at her age, or soon after, so I think we should just let the young girl make her own way,' Margaret replied.

Joe took his courage in his hands and approached the bevy of beauties. No small feat.

'Would you girls like a drink?'

It wasn't clear if he had thought out the effect on his meagre pay packet that nine drinks, even subsidised ones, would have.

The hum of chat and banter in the bar was interrupted by O'Rourke's raised voice. 'No can do,' he replied to Joe's slightly unsteady order for the girls' drinks. The barman then explained to the girls that their preferred choice of wine could not be delivered. 'Sold the last of it. Maybe it's Cumiskey's or the Hole in the Wall you're looking for.'

The lads, at the end of the bar, looked on haplessly, just glad not to be in Joe's shoes. Joe had done the right thing, the thing they should or could or might have done. He had broken the ice for them, but this might be a case of who dares doesn't win.

'As I was telling the civilians already, we are not really a wine-selling establishment.' O'Rourke had the attention of the room, and Joe was crimson red in the face at this point.

The girls were murmuring among themselves. The

gist of it was that the Hole in the Wall was walking distance from the barracks.

Blondie intervened: 'Girls, come on, we're settled here now. Let's stay.' This was code for *I already fancy one, or more, of the uniforms*. But at least Joe had an ally to mitigate his blushes.

'Come on, ladies, I haven't got all day, you know,' said Jimmy. No better man than O'Rourke to supervise a deteriorating atmosphere.

Fionn, having shaken off his trance-like state, now appeared among the girls. He was a much-needed ally for his embattled friend. 'You have red wine,' Fionn said calmly but assertively to O'Rourke.

It was Jimmy's turn to turn red, except his redness signalled a pending explosion.

'You have a case of Chateau Musar from the Bekaa Valley,' said Fionn.

This wasn't the Fionn that Joe knew. Joe had experienced some queer things, near misses and scrapes with him over their adolescent years, but this was a different Fionn.

The undivided attention of the packed mess now focused on the unholy tangle at the bar.

'Bekaa Valley me arse,' boomed O'Rourke. 'Now order or move on.'

'There is a case of Chateau Musar in the cold room,' insisted Fionn.

'Two things, sonny: one, how would you know what's in my cold room, and two, I have no intention of lifting the hatch to find out.' He was referring to the hatch door in the floor that led to the storage area for the beer kegs and bottles, cellars being another useful leftover from British military design of Irish Army barracks.

The leader of the girls' exit campaign was pushing harder for a move. You could read in her a lack of interest in boys, or at least the boys in this company. The tinder was smouldering, and if Camp Commandant O'Mahony had been present, he might have been wondering how a platoon with a peacekeeping mission would get on with belligerent, tribal Arabs if they couldn't handle Jimmy O'Rourke.

Margaret got up now and moved towards the action. 'Mr O'Rourke, Mr O'Rourke, would you please do me a favour? Would you please just let one of the young lads go and look?'

Even O'Rourke struggled to find a smart way of saying no to her disarmingly simple request.

With Jimmy O's jaw still hanging open, Margaret pushed home her advantage. 'Just do what he asks. I've seen him in these queer moods before, but he wouldn't put a fly wrong.'

O'Rourke bent down to grab the recessed metal handle of the hatch and raised it on its hinges. 'Be my guest,' was the best he could muster.

Fionn switched his attention to two of the young country lads from the platoon, Larry and Michael. The boys moved on whatever understanding Fionn's gaze had conveyed. They were at the end of the bar that was open, and they quickly proceeded behind the counter and down the ladder to the cellar.

With the girls' drinks on hold O'Rourke went back to dispensing pints while awaiting his vindication.

Margaret placed her hand on her son's shoulder as she negotiated her way back to Mary and Dermot. The heat she felt during the touch brought back a strange memory that reminded her of simpler days, rearing a young boy and recognising when you felt his brow that he was running a temperature. 'Is it really my time now?' she thought she heard her son say.

When she returned to the table, Margaret was greeted by Dermot trying to be humorous.

'Only bar I've ever been in where a man could die of thirst. Fair play to the lads for standing up to that eejit. And you too, Maggie.'

'There'll be wine in that cellar if Fionn said there was,' Margaret said.

'Ah come on, Maggie, how would he know that? I liked to see the lads taking on Goliath, but I don't think they'll be knocking him down.'

'I'm telling you, Dermot, I've seen my boy in that state before. It's like he goes into a meditation, or something like that. He said the strangest thing to me there. He said something about his time has come.'

'Ah for God's sake, Maggie, who does he think he is, the bleedin' Prophet Isaiah?'

Mary piped up to stop her husband getting hyper, 'Your Fionn does look pale, all right, but you know him and Joe will always stand up for each other. They'll be all right together abroad.'

The hum of conversation was rising in the room

as normality returned. Then there was a burst of applause and a few 'Well done, boys!'

Those closest to the bar were the first to see Michael step off the ladder, one hand firmly gripping the rope handle of an elegant wooden case. When Larry emerged, the two boys were able to present the case on the counter with a flourish. And there it was: a pristine, dust-covered case of Chateau Musar. O'Rourke's jaw dropped even lower than it had when Margaret disarmed him.

Taylor Brunswick, the platoon messer, occasionally experienced a spark of inspiration. In a put-on deep baritone he started singing, 'Oh happy day, Oh happy day, Oh happy day, Oh happy day.' He was bluffing, of course, and only knew the chorus, but he'd guessed correctly that the songstresses would join in. They couldn't help themselves. Not to be outdone and all that.

'When Jesus washed/ When Jesus washed/ Oh when He washed/ When Jesus washed/ He washed my sins away/ Oh happy day.'

Happy days as the boys and girls mingled and sang. Even the comb-overs had to join in.

While O'Rourke continued in his zombie-like state, the boys slid open the wine case cover and quickly uncorked two of the twelve gleaming bottles. O'Rourke was in no state to either call a halt to the singing or charge for the drinks. You could hardly charge for a product you didn't know you had. The mutiny was over and the party was on. The bullying O'Rourke was mumbling something. A Christian might say he was joining in with 'Good King Wenceslas' but it was doubtful.

A party, and a Christmas party at that. The Hole in the Wall would have to wait for another night. Fionn seemed to float out of the good-natured scrum at the bar and over to his mother's table.

'Well done, son, good job,' Margaret said.

'What trickery were you and my Joe up to, giving that excuse for a barman his comeuppance?' asked Dermot.

'I meant no harm,' Fionn said. 'I think I'll sit with you for a while.' He seemed visibly drained again after the bit of excitement.

'He gets like that after these queer episodes,' said Margaret, talking about him as if he wasn't there.

'I just want to enjoy the singing,' said Fionn as he rested his eyes, his back to the bar and his front to the fire.

Chapter **Two**

The week before departure to Fort Shamrock in the Lebanon was a break for the lads. Youngsters as they were, they had a natural inclination to enjoy the down time, especially after two tough, sodden months of training. Also, a reportedly bleak station awaited them in their desert camp. Even at this time of year you could be roasting by day and freezing by night.

Blondie had turned out to be a Miss Eleanor O'Brien. The initial attraction that had signalled a gravitational pull towards Joe had been cemented in the officers' mess. After the engagement with the enemy – Jimmy O'Rourke – the cement had set with a wine-induced kiss. Multiple kisses, really, outside the mess as the partygoers had dissipated into the fog that rolled off the Phoenix Park.

The two kids had had a couple of dates during the week. Joe's hormones were in disarray. He liked the look of this one as a keeper, but a nine-month absence was about to begin. He needn't have stressed himself, though. Girls need an emotional bond to develop before an intimate one can. Lads on the other hand want the sex part first, before forming an emotional connection. Nothing was happening below the waist, just because Joe was on a transporter the following Saturday. It would have to be enough for Joe to console himself that he had a good catch to think about while he was away. Eleanor seemed interested in him and not put off by his deployment. Letters would be the method of communication between the couple for the foreseeable future, and not French ones.

Fionn was very withdrawn in the week before leaving. He'd admitted to his mother that he was spending a bit of time in Victories church that week. He meant Our Lady of Victories, which was walking distance from their house.

'Are you going to Mass, son?' Margaret had asked.

'No, just enjoying the quiet and the light. The light through the stained-glass windows is beauty itself.'

Margaret didn't want to think about mental illness. She had always known Fionn might be the type to succumb. He was different. Him becoming a soldier occurred only by the accident of taking Joe's lead. Joe had chosen it as the easiest way to see at least a bit of the world. She knew Irish soldiers had been killed on peacekeeping missions, but that wasn't Margaret's biggest worry. Most of her siblings had had little bouts of mental unwellness, usually involving some time in hospital. Margaret had been lucky not to have been afflicted herself. She saw how the 'process' of it had affected her brothers and sisters: overwhelmed, hospitalised, six weeks of treatment, recovery. Quite effective, really, but still not something you would want for your son, and certainly not if getting stuck on medication for life was the upshot.

Fionn and Joe had emerged from the new middle classes. Their Dubliner parents had come from the working-class estates like Cabra, Drimnagh and Finglas that were built in the nineteen-fifties and sixties. They had all fought their way through the system and, at least to the outsider, had stepped up a rung of the ladder. The problem with being middle-class, or middle anything, is that you might be able to go up, but you can also go down.

There was a difference between parents like Dermot and Mary and their millennial sons like Joe. 'Too much minding and molly-coddling and not enough building resilience,' Dermot was prone to saying.

'You do need to make your own way through life, you know?' was a common refrain, even from Mary.

In fairness Dermot and Mary were not the worst example of millennial minding. They at least had not fallen into the trap of bludgeoning their offspring into the college system, with the hidden objective of massaging their own egos.

'Let him learn from himself,' Dermot had told Mary.

Mary agreed to follow Dermot's lead on this one. If it didn't work out, though, there might be hell to pay.

Margaret was relieved of any of this deep parental angst about steering her son in the right direction. Fionn had developed an independent, but not selfish, approach to life. He had been like this for the longest time.

Margaret recalled getting a note home from Fionn's teacher when he was seven, berating the child for not trying hard enough. Margaret had gently asked Fionn for the story behind the note and got a very good sounding of what was to come. Fionn had described how an older class had been invited into his junior classroom to witness a spelling competition among the kids. A few of the youngsters had volunteered to tackle the words randomly selected out of the hat. They had acquitted themselves well in front of the older boys. Hoping to finish with a flourish, the teacher had sought a final volunteer but had been met with an embarrassing silence, which caused her to redden a little. Fionn stepped forward, but the words, *hippopotamus*, for example, did not hold his interest, and one out of five was not the triumphant conclusion Miss Mills had been hoping for. Hence the note.

'Teacher finished off at the bell for lunch by saying that all the class had done very well, all except for Fionn O'Toole.'

'I'd say that left you in a miserable mood, son, and I'll be writing back to that Mills one.'

'No need, Ma, she was misguided, that's all. The good spellers went first and did a good job. And so what? I wasn't bothered at all. She was just wrong.'

That little incident marked the start of a shift in the mother–son relationship. Margaret kept as nice a home as she could on her meagre income, and Fionn was going to turn that to his advantage. He was only looking upwards.

There had been incidents during their early and teenage years that had caused Joe to wonder just what made his friend tick. Was it that Fionn took the lead because no one else would, or was it some other form of over-compensation for those around him? Joe admired his buddy but knew that, too often, he was happy to take the shortcut of rowing in behind Fionn's lead. This seemed to him to be a natural response when someone else was willing to do the heavy lifting, but his dad always encouraged him to stand up and be counted.

The first time Joe noticed a power in Fionn was when they were eight years old. There can be a viciousness in small kids that's so unsavoury that adults convince themselves 'That would never have been me.' The classroom bullies made a target of Fionn, who came across as a bit different. Fionn was having none of it and had no problem dealing with their teasing. He simply ignored them and took himself out of earshot. This irked the ringleader, Eric.

Eric the Terrible had decided to sort this Fionn fella out once and for all. The bullies had cleverly employed an agent to do their bidding. A big autistic lad, maybe ten or eleven years of age, was encouraged to lie in wait behind a wall near the school gates. The smaller brains behind the operation had demonstrated how all would be well in the world if he would just smash the rock he had been armed with into Fionn's face.

Eric and two runts diverted Joe from Fionn's side to facilitate the ambush, and before he could do anything, Joe saw his friend lying on the ground with a much larger boy standing with his feet planted either side of Fionn's stomach. The assailant held the rock in both hands above his head.

From nowhere appeared a sight that none of the youngsters were used to seeing – a lone garda on foot patrol. The burly assailant could only deal with order, and having a stranger grab his shoulder while at the same time unleashing an unmerciful roar in his ear was not at all orderly.

Fionn seemed to anticipate what would happen next – that the stone would be unwittingly, out of fright, be dropped in the direction of his privates. It was, and without any fuss, he simply caught the rock in his two hands and laid it to one side.

Diminutive Eric was the next to feel the long arm of the law … literally. The young, skinny garda must have had a sense of what was afoot. He gave Eric an enthusiastic open-palmed clatter to the cheek, which knocked Eric on his arse. Thankfully, for the garda, in the Dublin suburbs of the mid-noughties, mobile phones and social media were not yet ubiquitous. If they had been, the guard and his clatter would surely have gone viral.

After that the bullies just didn't feature, neither annoying Fionn nor anyone else. Eric either lost his passion for evil leadership or saw the error of his ways.

As Joe looked back, he compiled a collection of little events from the boys' teenage years. Once they were robbing an orchard, when Farmer Jack set upon them, cursing like blue murder. Like a trapped frog, covering his eyes in the hope that the danger would disappear, Joe knew he was done for when he ran, only to find a high-walled cul-de-sac at the end of the orchard. The thin trunks of the apple trees didn't provide many opportunities for avoiding detection. But Farmer Jack walked right by a crouching Joe. A great, slightly inexplicable, escape.

Fionn avoided aggravation throughout his adolescence, but Joe could remember one time when his friend resorted to violence. Fionn didn't do sport growing up but Joe did; he had the teenage testosterone for it. Soccer was an opportunity for him to get out from under Fionn's wing, something his father encouraged. The match results were OK, but some of the company was a bit dodgy. Within the under-sixteen ranks, an opportunity to sell marijuana presented itself to a budding entrepreneur. Joe inhaled and confided in Fionn that it made him vomit. At the very next training session, Fionn joined in, after a fashion. When the boys got together behind the clubhouse for their post-training joint, Fionn was there. The joint was being passed along, and Fionn waited and took his turn. In the quickest move Joe ever saw him make, he pinned Gavin to the wall and viciously stubbed the lit end into his cheek. The smell of burning skin shook the team out of their stupor and the rescue of a smouldering Gavin was executed. Joe hurriedly led Fionn away before he could be set upon. Fionn was never invited back, but neither was the would-be drug lord. The dalliance with drugs had been stubbed out by wanton violence.

The army was a different thing, though, and in some ways it further rebalanced the friendship between Joe and Fionn. Joe was out of his friend's shadow again. This time Fionn was the follower and all was good with the double act again. Joe felt good that he could be 'the man' for a change. But something would happen during army training that would make Joe rethink who the man really was.

Chapter **Three**

Both now in their forties, the two sergeants had been to the Lebanon before, Kevin Doyle twice and Martin O'Brien three times. They knew the ropes, as it were, even though this time was a little unusual, to say the least. The platoon was only thirteen strong, with no lieutenant and no corporals. The sergeants, to their credit, didn't mind the absence of a lieutenant. In a way that could be seen as a compliment. Regarding the corporals, the commandant insisted that some would earn corporals' stripes during the nine months of the tour.

'Whoever shines through,' he said.

Two things bugged the sergeants. One, it would be the first time they had to mind a bunch of kids without having a wily old hack of a corporal, on the inside, telling them what was going on. Secondly, and much more importantly, they knew that the mission was a new one and a strange one at that. They were landing in Jordan. The first time for Irish peacekeepers.

'Cutbacks me hole,' was Martin's take on it. They knew such a small outfit would mean twenty-four-hour stints of sentry duty instead of twelves. The justification for keeping the platoon small was secrecy, apparently. Fewer soldiers to blabber, even though their orders were that the mission's location would be revealed only upon landing at their destination. Even then, the privates' families would be told only that there was a change of location, not the actual new location.

'All a bit cloak and dagger,' was Kevin's opinion.

Why all the kids, though, and a girl? They both pondered on that one.

Martha had been absent with permission on the night of the infamous mess battle christened 'O'Rourke's Drift'.

She made light of Fionn's antics: 'No matter. I'm a white-wine drinker anyhow.' She probably would have been feisty enough to cut off O'Rourke herself, if she had been there to witness his unmannerly treatment of the boys.

Martha had warmed to Fionn because of the decent and natural way he behaved around her during their basic training. She knew, the way girls know, that this was a platonic gig. She just hadn't figured out if that was what she wanted.

Martha took on the inevitable role of being tougher than the lads as the representative of women in a man's world. The other young fellas were finding their feet in dealing with a female private. Private Jake Hardiman had already made the mistake of taking her on in a verbal joust, making sure there were plenty around to hear.

'Martha, have you ever been mistaken for a man?'

'No. Have you?'

That shut Jake up for a while, and guys who sniggered at the put-down also had their cards marked.

'Jake, that didn't go so well,' said Fionn.

'Ah, for God's sake, I was only having a laugh,' said a blushing Jake.

'Yeah, but it's a laugh at another human being's expense, and maybe they're not the best laughs. You can be a man without trying to be The Man for an audience,' said Fionn. He wasn't finished. 'You know, I often think that's where mental illness comes from – a person trying to be something that will be accepted. Whatever happened to people being themselves, being the best their parents brought them up to be? Jake, be yourself, and as for you, Taylor, I know your game.'

'Ah here, don't go picking on me,' Taylor said.

'All that trick-acting and pretending to be a clown. You have good in ye in spades. Let it out, why don't ye?' said Fionn.

The two young boys had never been spoken to like that by an adult, never mind a peer.

Both sergeants were impressed by young Fionn. They agreed that he was certainly different, mature for a twenty-year-old, sure of his opinions. He already seemed to be the leader of the young boys and girl private.

Sergeant O'Brien had recommended to the commandant that Private Fionn be appointed corporal of the platoon before the tour. 'No deal,' the CO instantly responded. He was suspicious that the sergeants' real motivation was to make life a little easier for themselves, not to mention having a chain-of-command scapegoat.

The CO was also a bit miffed over that case of Chateau Musar that had fallen into enemy hands. He was sure that must have been a forgotten present sent by some Lebanese mayor or official. His view was that any stripe-holder or potential stripe-holder didn't go in for any messing that defrauded an officer of his rightful due. In any event he was genuinely concerned as to whether a twenty-year-old kid could handle the three older career privates in the platoon. He had a point. If the youngster got his spirit broken by the older guys, he'd be turned off soldiering for life.

Unlike Martha, the older privates hadn't seen Fionn in action during basic training in the Glen of Imaal. The plan was that the eight new recruits would be trained by the sergeants for seven weeks. They were then joined by the three career soldiers for the last week of basic training so that the unit could bond as a functioning platoon before they departed.

Being billeted away from family for two months answered a couple of questions. First, could the kids be taught how to fire a gun, do hand-to-hand combat, be real soldiers? Second, had they the bottle to live away from Mammy's apron strings for more than a few days? The latter was important because if you whinged enough in the hills of wintery Wicklow, you could at least be discharged, unfit for military duty, and be home in hours. If, however, you made it to a foreign station, that was a different matter. You might be a youngster, but you would be subject to military law. Bailing out would mean court martial and a dishonourable discharge.

That September and October in Wicklow were bleak for the recruits. The ground underfoot was sodden towards the end of autumn and this was felt in the weight of the army-issue boots, as the hillside mud crusted their soles. The barracks, where night-time exhaustion was treated with lights out at ten, were a standard dormitory affair. Military regulation allowed for a curtained partition for the female soldiers. No airs and graces here.

There probably would have been a lot more moaning about pay except there was nowhere to spend the miserly remuneration of a basic soldier. There was also the lure of the serving-overseas allowance, which meant that the Christmas period – not this one but the next one – would be a time of plenty.

Training itself was tough to the point of brutality. The drill was to break down the spirit until orders become unquestionable. There was also the unifying threat that if one soldier failed in anything, all soldiers would be punished.

Sergeants O'Brien and Doyle were a good double act. They knew they were stuck in the Glen training ground for eight solid weeks. Solid was meant to mean 24/7. The sergeants had formed their own private pact. They would both be there during the day but would take alternate nights off for family time. This was the Irish Army after all, not the US Marines boot camp in Parris Island.

The men ended every training day with a whiskey at six o'clock, to accompany their debriefing at which they discussed who was showing enough spirit to warrant their attention. Spirit had to be, if not broken, at least fashioned. If you had to order a soldier to attack a mortar position, the last thing you wanted was a spirited discussion: *Why me? Why don't you do it?*

These were dyed-in-the-wool army guys. They trained their troops hard by day, knowing they were doing them a favour. There was nothing to do at night in the bleakness of the remote Wicklow hills, so you may as well be exhausted and bed down.

Eight weeks of basic training was enough to get a good read on the enlisted men under you. You had to know what personality type you could rely on. Sure, the training was designed to get the boys to take and obey orders. But also the question of who you would give a detail to, knowing that they could be relied upon, had to be answered.

The sergeants took turns roaring at their soldiers during endless fitness and endurance drills in the mud. No exceptions were made for Martha, either. She could sink or swim. After four weeks it was clear what the group dynamic was.

The lads from the country – Paul Devitt, Michael Moriarty and Larry Duffy – were tough, reliable sorts. Paul was from a military family anyway. The Dubliners were an assorted mix. Jake was the quiet man of the party. Taylor was a joker, but there was no malice in his foolery. Martha was a girl making her way in a man's world. Joe and Fionn had history. They were thick and had every intention of looking out for each other. It was up to the sergeants to mould that bond to their advantage.

Fionn had leadership written all over him. Simple things impressed the sergeants. He'd pick up on anyone who was struggling on a particular day and would stick close by, to shore them up. That was something O'Brien and Doyle knew could make the difference between losing your way as a trainee soldier and making it.

Doyle and O'Brien were career soldiers. They knew they were alike in not always seeing eye to eye with the commissioned officers. No problem on this mission, so, as there were none. In their private conversations, though, they discussed something that was bugging them in relation to being chosen for a new type of mission. The secrecy was one thing. Their destination – Bethlehem, via Jordan – was top secret. Crossing swords with the Israeli military was courting trouble, as many Irish soldiers knew from their experiences in Lebanon. It was absolutely necessary to keep the wool pulled over their squad's eyes while they could still communicate with their families.

Then there was the squad, the platoon and its make-up. Had somebody thought this out? For all the world it looked too stupid to be incompetent. The sergeants knew full well that their older three privates had, let's say, reputations that preceded them. On top of that there were the kids, eight of them, one of them a female private heading to a Muslim country. In the sergeant's eyes something wasn't adding up. But orders are orders and egos are egos. If the two men could pull off this mission, they would be applauded by the entire Irish military family and beyond.

Chapter **Four**

It had been a God-sent misty day in the hills of the platoon's training camp. The group were together but would be sergeant-less for the training exercise ahead. All the remaining eleven were charged with orienteering so that they would avoid enemy contact. The enemy in this case being a team of experienced army rangers from Camp Imaal. What the sergeants were hoping for was that the platoon would route in an exaggerated fashion to avoid the enemy. Better still if they lost the light, and a further bonus if they had to spend the night in the mountains. Now that would sort the men from the boys and girl, O'Brien thought. He had seen it before with the new breed of youngsters signing up. They tackled compass work with the idea that they'd always have their smartphones for back-up.

'Not if it runs out of signal, ye won't,' he told them.

'Did it before,' piped up Private Pete.

The new recruits had met Peter, Mark and Seamus just three days previously. At least Pete was up for it. All Mark and Seamus had prattled on about since they'd met was how long they'd been in. Fourteen years in one case and twelve in the other, and how long they had to go till pension, twenty-one years' service. Funnily enough, though, none of the three had seen peacekeeping duty before.

Larry, Michael and Paul had formed a little company within the platoon. They had the common bond of being from the country – Donegal, Tralee and Athlone respectively.

Paul's father had been a sergeant serving out of Athlone Barracks. He had seen UN service himself in the seventies, which now seemed like a lifetime ago. Even further back was his grandad, a soldier in the fifties. Paul's dad, another Paul, used to refer to it as 'back in old God's time'. Young Paul, through his dad, knew a lot more than the other kids about soldiering. More to the point, he had the inside track on what to expect from the older enlisted men. Sergeant Paul was an older father, a much older one who had Paul junior after he married a woman thirty years younger than him. He was a product of love, nonetheless, and Paul wanted to do well for his mam and dad.

Young Paul had been warned off the Three Stooges, as his father had referred to the older privates. They were career good-for-nothings, to be avoided, according to his father. 'Those three being allowed to influence young soldiers is the epitome of an army regime gone mad. Why in my day …' etc., etc. He had earned the right. He had seen life-and-death soldiering.

Paul junior, not surprisingly for a twenty-two-year-old, was happy to use his own judgement. He thought Private Pete was at least worth giving a chance to. Pete was from Mullingar, another midlands man.

'Listen, lads,' Peter had advised the platoon in advance of their orienteering hike, 'the one thing we want to avoid is running into the rangers. They're tough bastards, the elite and all that. They'd do a week's training and then follow up with a triathlon at the weekend.'

'Yeah, bastards all right,' Private Mark pitched in. 'Those feckers will end up clogging up the medical system in years to come with their bad knees and matching bad backs.'

'Why should we be bothered, though?' asked Private Jake.

'Because their instructions are to rough us up if they catch us in the hills. And I mean a good hiding,' Mark said.

'And by the way, Miss Martha, they won't be making any allowance for sex, not before they give ye a couple of pucks in the mouth.'

Martha was ready to tough it out. 'Yeah, but not before I stick one of them with a good kick in the bollix,' she said.

Peter, Mark and Seamus were revelling in the conversation, in being shown a bit of respect and being listened to. Private Seamus was next to row in: 'Fair enough, Martha, but Mark is right – we're better off giving the rangers a wide berth. We've done these hikes before. The weight of the boots on your feet is leaden with the caked-on muck. Ye might be struggling to walk with the exhaustion of it, never mind raising your leg for a kung fu kick.'

Suited and booted and laden down with full packs, off the gang of eleven went into the darkness of the Wicklow hills, at 7 a.m., on into the mist of a crisp late October morning.

'Jaysus, why all the extra rations of food?' was Martha's last comment as the sergeant-less squad started its walk and ended its debate.

Peter replied in a conciliatory tone of voice: 'You're still not following the plot, girl. They're hoping to feck that we are out all night.'

It was the week before Halloween. There's always an atmosphere about Halloween in the countryside and towns of Celtic countries. The changing of the seasons, the Ka of the dark spirits and the mischief of the otherworld is all around.

Heading uphill into thickening fog lent itself to the edgy atmosphere. Visibility was down to about fifty metres. The compensation was that at least a ranger was unlikely to frighten the shite out of you by jumping out of nowhere. Simply because, if you were silent, he wasn't going to find you.

Private Pete, assuming command, sent out a whispered message to be passed along through each soldier in the diagonally arranged platoon: 'No loud voices. Sound carries in the fog and that's the only way the rangers can catch ye.'

The group, although not carrying rifles, were proceeding in battle formation. Ten metres apart, up and down dale. It was bloody tiring, and all the time building to a crunch point when the tension of the exercise would be overtaken by fatigue.

Pete took up the central position in the formation, with Seamus and Mark at the lead and end flanks. They could both see Pete but not each other, and it seemed a good idea to keep the youngsters in between them. The group had so far only stopped for one break – water, tea flask and high-energy bars at noon. You could see the shape of the heatless sun above the fog. Fionn and Joe used the break to chatter away with Martha. She had aligned herself more with the two boys as the training had progressed. Martha liked the way Fionn stayed quiet until he had something to say. It was almost as if he was conserving energy. Joe was more inclined to feel awkward with silence and to fill the space with chit chat.

Pete had insisted that the boys didn't start fucking around with maps and compasses. 'We know the route the rangers will take. They'll go around the Glen, jogging in a circumference. We'll go over the top of Imaal. They are banking on staying on the lower ground and spotting or hearing us with the better visibility lower down.'

The Glen of Imaal was, apart from being the Irish Army's training ground, a lonely parcel of boggy hills that made up part of the Wicklow Mountains. If you got lost and isolated, you'd be in trouble quicker than you expected.

By four-thirty in the afternoon, with the sky not looking so bright, Pete was feeling uneasy in the way that you give half your senses over to feeling queer and the other half over to telling yourself that everything will be all right. He was still convincing himself that they were taking the right route. After all, they had been heading downhill for the last forty-five minutes. He couldn't communicate with Mark or Seamus without giving his hand away. Pete's unease was over whether they had taken a wrong turn or not. To console himself further he was thinking, I won't be talking flak from any fuckers who wouldn't take the lead if their life depended on it.

While Pete was stuck in his reverie, the silent drudgery was broken by a high-pitched moan that he determined to have come from close to his left.

'Oh, please God, please God, tell me no, tell me no.'

Pete broke formation and moved quickly twenty metres to his left, passing Jake. 'What the fuck is up with you?' he said.

'It was just there, the red tip, the red tip,' said Paul.

'What red tip?' asked Pete as the rest of the platoon joined them, initially glad of the diversion.

'A fucking shell, a fucking shell, a fucking shell, a fucking shell,' Paul shouted as if they were the only words he knew or could say.

'Jesus, Mary and Joseph,' Mark screeched. He was already involuntarily backing down the hill away from the ad-hoc circle that had formed around the commotion. 'The one fucking thing you eejits are told, the one fucking thing, is that you steer a mile clear of unexploded ordinance. It's the only fucking rule of the training ground.' Mark was now fifteen metres away and still slowly backing away. He was close enough to hear Paul's stammering response to his accusation.

'You're looking down, always looking for a solid foothold in the muck. You see something that looks solid to stand on it, that's all. A fucking shell.' The colour had drained from Paul's cheeks and beads of sweat were visible on his forehead. His blood pressure would be dropping now as shock set in. His brain was trying to glue together a justification for the mistake. He couldn't just take his foot off the shell tip. It was flight or fright, and this was definitely fright. By now his foot had sunk a good three inches into the muck and would take a fair effort to extract.

Fionn took a step forward towards Pete and Paul. Joe took half a step in solidarity. The rest were in stupor mode except for the ever-retreating Mark who was now thirty-five metres down the hill.

Fionn looked directly at Pete and asked, 'What's going on?'

'Nothing fucking good.'

'Pete, come on, I need you to be thinking clearly.' Fionn's authoritative tone seemed to have the desired effect.

'Once there is pressure applied to a shell head, it will blow.'

'I need you to tell me what that means here, for us.'

'Look, if he is standing on a live shell head, the pressure is already releasing a phosphorous charge into the detonation chamber. So it's going to blow anyway. The more pressure the quicker the bang.'

'Then why don't we pull his leg out and run?' Fionn asked.

'For fuck's sake, Fionn, that shell hit the ground spinning. Some small defect in the casing. God knows what condition it's in. That's if it is a shell. Maybe the idiot stood on a flattened Coke can or something red.'

At least now the gang had something hopeful to cling on to, but the faces in the ten-metre-wide circle were still ashen.

'OK,' said Fionn, 'so here's how we go. I need one pair of additional hands to help and I need those hands to be nimble.'

He was looking at Martha. Her lips, which were slightly parted, emitted a dry sound that could be interpreted as a 'yeah'.

'Pete, you and the lads back away to a safe distance.'

The circle was now growing in a gentle radius of retreat. Some heading up, some down. Pete, who was not willing to desert his command without some form of mock protest, asked, 'What's the plan?'

Fionn demonstrated: 'I'm going to hold Paul's boot firmly down, applying pressure, like this, while Martha gently digs out the muck around the boot.'

Pete had only been asking for an explanation, not a demonstration He was glad when Fionn repeated, 'Go on, Pete, move them back.'

Now there were three. Paul was shaking slightly, with shock. Only he was in a position to see the retreating figures turn into ghostlike shapes in the fog and gathering murky darkness.

'Martha, dig away with those gentle hands and keep the heavy muck together. I'll keep the pressure on, and when I can pull Paul's foot out, you'll replace it with the muck, right into the boot. All good?'

'Me dad is going to kill me if I get blown up,' Paul said.

Martha was looking at Fionn and could have sworn she caught him smiling at the unintentional black humour. It lightened her mood enough for her to say, 'Maybe it is just a Coke can.'

'Yeah, maybe,' Fionn said.

Paul was crying gently now, still shivering. Four minutes of gingerly executed work gave them a good pile of heavy Wicklow muck. Fionn used his left hand to press down on Paul's uncovered boot.

'Martha, undo the laces.'

Their heads were in danger of clashing as they both worked at Paul's feet. Fionn used his right hand and arm to lift out Paul's stockinged foot.

'Right, my man, you're free. Off you go.'

By this stage Paul was incapable of talking. Lazarus-like, he walked off down the hill, with one stockinged foot squelching, to join the ghosts.

The dull orange flash stunned everyone. Stones and muck landed on and about them. They were all on the ground suddenly, not knowing if they were there because of a voluntary or involuntary action. The noise of the blast seemed to send the fog down the mountain in an avalanche that culminated in total silence. Then the dawning realisation: I might be alive, but life will never be the same. I was there when soldiers in my platoon died, were maimed, were not whole, were brave, were stupid, were on the nine o'clock news.

Oh my fucking God, oh God, Pete was thinking, delaying the decision to move to the blast site. There was some kind on movement up ahead.

Seamus bellowed, 'Get up here, all of ye, quick!'

The circle converged in the gloom.

'Jaysus, that's what I'd call a hole, all right,' said Taylor, maybe not knowing what else to say.

'It's called a crater,' Pete said angrily, wondering why nobody was trying to solve the bloody mystery of the missing bodies.

The faces around the blast site were stupefied.

Not put off by Pete's abruptness, Taylor couldn't help himself. 'Were they blown to bits?'

Pete had had enough and gave him a full force thump in the arm. Taylor let out a moan, as the group tried to process the tragedy. Could it be that there was nothing left of them? How would anyone know? They were soldiers, mostly kids, and all of them got their knowledge of wounds and bombs from Hollywood.

Pete tried to think, but his brain was fried by what had just taken place. Was it appropriate to even be thinking?

'A dead soldier girl will be a hard story for the army to sell.'

Joe had tears in his eyes. He had moved on to a scene, in his head, where he was standing in front of Fionn's mother.

The stupor ended kind of gently. Fionn was standing directly behind Pete now. Pete had only been alerted to this by the lads, and particularly Seamus, who were standing upslope on the hill directly across from the crater. Seamus was wide-eyed. This was noticeable even in the growing darkness because of the way the whites of eyes always stand out when faces have camouflage polish smeared across them. That was the first thing Pete noticed when he turned to face Fionn. Both his and Martha's faces were clean.

Pete shoved Taylor out of the way and proceeded to perform the most instinctual hug he had ever been driven to deliver. The hug wasn't entirely successful because Fionn himself clutched Martha to his side, holding her firmly around the shoulder. As Pete threw his outstretched arms around the pair, he noticed how firmly Fionn was holding on to Martha. He was keeping her upright.

'What the fuck? Are you all right? Where did you come from?' Pete blurted as he released them.

The rest of the lads came to take a closer look, steering around the hole in the ground, euphoria rising in all of them. Rowdiness and shouting were OK now. Relief. Fuck the rangers.

The lads saw that back-slapping was in order, and Joe was next to embrace Fionn. Hugging wasn't something that was common among Irish young fellas but given the circumstances it was needed as a tension reliever. Fionn returned the embrace as he knew Larry and Michael were on hand to buttress Martha from falling. Farming lads always had more biological sense, like that, about them. Paul and Martha had been two of the main actors in the drama, but only Fionn was able to talk and take in the group's relieved congratulations.

Taylor, still holding his sore arm, spoke up: 'Lads, I suppose I'll be getting another thump soon. The rangers will have heard that bang, right?'

Pete was now more conciliatory: 'No worries on that score. Those boys keep office hours. They'll be snug in their bunks tonight.'

'We will be as well, right?' asked Taylor.

Pete called Mark and Seamus over to him. 'Boys, I think we'll hole up here for the night. What do ye reckon?' The two just grunted so Pete carried on. 'I was crouched at a position only fifty metres directly below us. We've been here before, but I only noticed now it's an old stone circle. Not much shelter but at least it's a boundary.'

'Sleeping in a fairy circle! It sure is turning out to be a day of queer experiences,' said Seamus.

Mark had one of his rare contributory moments. 'Yeah, OK,' he said. 'It'll give us time to get our story straight.'

Seamus wasn't letting him off the hook so lightly. 'Is that the story where you were the first to beat a retreat down the bloody hill?'

'How many dead heroes were you planning to clock up?' Mark replied.

'Ah give up, give up, for fuck's sake!' said Pete. He was more annoyed by not being able to figure out the geometry of how Fionn and Martha had ended up standing behind him.

'Let's move the boys down and get a fire going. There're only a few minutes of daylight left. These two' – Peter pointed at Paul and Martha – 'need to be minded – shock. Let's get going.'

Pete continued to use Larry and Michael to help marshal the dazed Martha and Paul, with his squelchy stockinged foot, down the hill. Fionn and Joe ambled behind. Joe wasn't talking but the stress pain in his stomach was easing. No-stripes Pete had a head on his shoulders. When he took off his backpack, he knew exactly where to look to retrieve a couple of paraffin-smelling firelighters wrapped in tin foil. Using a small Bic lighter and the couple of twigs he had collected on the way down the hill, he soon had the beginnings of a camp fire.

'Larry, Michael, will you park those two here beside the fire and do a bit of wood gathering.' Pete wasn't anti-Dublin, but he instinctively trusted the country lads, like himself, to be more cooperative.

It was dark now and Pete got a bit of a blaze going, which encouraged the rest of the troops to congregate in the circle. He had ringed the fire with a cordon of stones – a stone circle within a stone circle.

With the troops gathered around Pete spoke: 'Boys,

it won't rain in a fog so your twenty-tog survival bags will keep ye snug.' There were a few moans when he confirmed that they were staying put for the night. 'The timber-gathering detail will be back soon and we'll get some grub cooked.'

'Have we any drink?' asked Taylor.

Pete knew he had been on Taylor's case enough, and anyway he was nearly wishing he had brought a flask. 'Let's concentrate on a sugar-restoring meal,' he said.

Martha and Paul got pride of place, close to the fire. The base of the mountain, where they were now, had a surprising amount of scattered wood when you went looking for it. Probably from a woodland that had existed a thousand years ago. In the glow of illuminated grey fog a little sense of normality had returned. Nothing like a tinned-beef dinner, heated on the fire, to return you to a state of quasi-normality. After what had just happened, things were going to be different. The lads were gathered in huddles. Fionn and Joe kept their own company, but it seemed to Pete that Joe was doing most of the talking. The kids had survived, literally, their first soldiering adventure. What was to come in the far-off hills of the Middle East could surely only be boring by comparison.

Not surprisingly, the older guys – Pete, Mark and Seamus – were gathered together, eating. Pete had positioned himself behind Martha and Paul. He was happy they were sitting up and eating a bit. Pete wanted to talk with Mark and Seamus and could see that a dazed Martha wouldn't be paying much heed to them.

'Lads, we're after surviving a near miss balls up,' said Pete.

'We're going to have to get our story straight for camp tomorrow,' said Seamus.

'You don't have to be a good liar if you're not telling the truth. You just have to remember to shut up,' Mark replied.

'I think the truth is the last thing we want to deal with right now,' said Pete.

'The truth, if you ask me, means no stripes, and do ye know what that means for your pension, Mark?' said Seamus.

Seamus had Mark's full attention, if not Pete's, once money was mentioned.

'So what is our story and how do we keep the kids from ratting?' asked Mark.

'One thing is for sure, boys, we'll have to figure out who's a blabberer and who can be trusted,' said Seamus.

'Lads, stall the ball awhile,' said Pete. 'No matter what, something very strange just happened. We're bonded as a platoon now, whether we know it or not. How are those two guys not dead or limbless or something?'

'That's obvious, isn't it? They weren't blown up,' said Mark, logical to a fault.

'Well, how then did they magically appear from nowhere with shiny clear faces?' asked Pete.

'Duh! Well, I'm guessing they walked away from the boot bomb, just like the rest of us, and cleaned themselves up for good measure,' said Mark a little smartly.

'Pete is right, Mark,' said Seamus.

'The timing is all wrong. Fionn and Martha couldn't have just walked through a ring of soldiers who were tensed up with adrenalin and on high alert.

'Lads, come on,' said Mark. 'It's spooky enough being out here in the Halloween fog, stone circles and what have you. Supernatural happenings me arse, if that's what you're getting at. They did their job and they walked away. Good night and God bless.'

'Stop being such a fucking smart-arse,' Seamus said to Mark, and he wasn't finished. 'Maybe the speed that got you down the hill yourself would have stopped you from seeing anything go past you.'

'Ah lads, give it a rest. It's hard enough figuring the thing out without a load of bickering,' said Pete.

'How did they get their faces so clean, no camouflage paint?'

'Ask them,' said Mark, tetchy again.

'Well, I will, because we can't put together a credible story for HQ till we know what happened,' said Pete.

'I'd ask the Martha one first, if I were you, Pete,' said Mark. 'That Fionn guy talks in riddles anyway.'

Pete manoeuvred closer to Martha but still within earshot of the older two privates. He needed their support. 'Martha, are you OK?' he asked.

'Not bad, Peter,' was her soft-spoken reply.

'Make sure you keep inside the bag. We can't have your temperature dropping. We should really have taken a closer look at ye for cuts or injuries. Martha, what do you remember about the explosion?'

'Flying, hitting, being dead,' was Martha's astonishing reply, more so because it was delivered in the same calm monotone as her previous sentence. With the three lads stuck for words, she carried on: 'I was lying on my back. I thought I was dead because the pain I felt when I hit the ground was the worst I've ever felt. And then I felt nothing. My eyes opened and there was no fog and Fionn was leaning over me and his hands were on my shoulders … and the heat. He said, 'Get up, Martha.'

'Oh, for fuck's sake,' said Mark. 'We're trying to get our story straight and she's talking about coming back from the dead. Listen Miss Mary or Martha or whatever your name is, quit talking shite, will ye, for Jaysus sake?'

'Lighten up, Mark,' said Pete. 'Can't you see the girl is shattered?'

The senior privates had chosen to interview Martha while most of the rest of the lads were pummelling Fionn for information. They were able to hear what Fionn was relating even as they sat, on their side of the fire, with Martha. Paul's chums, Larry and Michael, were keeping Paul chatting and distracted.

'That was one hell of a job you did today, my man,' Joe said to Fionn. He wasn't expecting much of a response; he never did after seeing Fionn do his thing.

But Joe knew this was more than just another 'thing'. This was unexplainable. So he asked Fionn directly: 'My friend, were you blown up in that explosion?'

'Lads, I don't really know how to explain it. It might sound a bit stupid. It wasn't so much that I was guided by nature, more that I was perfectly in tune with it. I'm not explaining it very well. When I was dealing with the bomb, I felt I was part of something. I knew I was guided and nothing could go wrong. It did – the bloody thing exploded – but even so, I knew me and Martha, because she was with me, were protected. There was a whole sense of well-being, as if the detonation happened to prove a point, or something.

'Fionn, are you saying you have special powers, or something? I'm confused,' Jake said.

'I don't know what I have, Jake, but I know I only want to do good with it.'

'So are you the man to ask about picking lottery numbers?' asked Taylor.

'I don't think it's that kind of good work I have to do, Taylor, my friend.'

'Fionn, did the blast blow you over everyone's head? We were all hiding well away,' said Jake.

'But who among us knows anything about bomb blasts? Even the older guys – you can ask them, but I don't know if they've seen many blasts either,' Fionn replied.

Paul was safely tucked up in his waterproof sleeping bag by the fire. His buddies approached and used the excuse of heaping some more wood on the fire to sit beside him, while Pete was talking with Martha.

'Jesus, man, you're the lucky boy to have only lost your boot,' said Larry.

'Yeah, right enough, could have lost your bollix,' said Michael.

This was as meek as the lads had ever seen Paul. His normal confidence, maybe brought on from knowing a bit more about the army, had evaporated for the moment.

'The bravery of these guys, Martha and Fionn, and the coolness of Fionn. I wonder, no matter how long we live, will we ever see such an act again,' said Paul, his voice quivering.

'Fionn's quite a lad, for a Dub, that is,' said Michael.

'Go way out of that, will ye! You Kerry lads love the feckin' Dubs,' said Larry.

'Yeah, love tanning their hides in football, more like,' Michael replied.

'Us Donegalers have done a little bit of that ourselves in recent times.'

'Boys, enough of the GAA shitting competition for the minute. I'm fucking lucky to have a pair of legs and your spitting and shitting on about sport.' Paul was getting himself way more hyper than was good for him.

'Yeah, you're right, Paul,' Larry said.

Michael nodded in agreement.

'But listen, fair play, Fionn's been nothing but a decent sort in the last eight weeks.'

'Bang on,' said Michael.

'Do you remember when Sarge Doyle told us that if anyone failed one of those crappy, late-evening endurance drills, then no one goes to bed till 4 a.m.? Sure enough, Jake was thirty seconds behind the pace with five minutes left on the clock. Ye remember Fionn and Joe grabbing him under each arm and beating the clock by a nick? Doyle was raging, ye remember? Not because he had it in for us but more because he was thwarted in keeping us up half the night. He wanted to see how we would react, how we would treat the one who let the squad down.'

'Yeah, Fionn was always thwarting the sarges,' said Larry.

'He just wouldn't leave anyone behind … as I just found out for myself, thank God,' said Paul, now a bit calmer.

'Yeah, and I like the way he just doesn't go in for that Dublin-versus-country shite,' said Michael.

'Maybe he's a born-again culchie,' said Larry.

'Yeah, but there is more to it than that, right enough. He treats us all equally.'

'Well, he treated me more than equally. He saved my life,' said Paul.

'I've news for ye, Paul, he might have saved your life, but he saved my bacon while he was at it,' said Larry.

'What ye mean?' asked Michael.

'He caught me carrying a flask of whiskey. I've no idea how he knew it, but he put his hand in my inside pocket, grabbed the flask, took a swig and emptied the lot, just before Sarge O'Brien called a bunk inspection. I would have been kicked out of the platoon.'

'Sweet Jesus, what are we to do with this balls-up?' Seamus asked, really addressing the senior privates.

'Lads, don't lose the plot here. At least with no dead bodies, thank God, we have options,' said Pete.

'Options to lie, ye mean,' replied Mark.

This group were talking more quietly than Fionn and Joe's.

'Jaysus, lads, this is huge. I think the bloody relief of us all not being splattered with blood is one thing. A good thing. But one way or the other this is going to follow us all for ever,' said Pete.

'Could two people be blown that far in the air and really come up unscathed?' asked Seamus.

'It's a crock of shit story, if you're asking me. Look, we were in a circular cordon around the blast site. Of course the boyos could have slipped past us, washed their faces and carried on with their trickery,' said Mark, getting crankier by the minute.

'Look, it's head-wrecking. I'm just saying we are in a better place than we could have been,' said Pete.

'I just wonder if we're making ourselves believe the unbelievable,' said Seamus.

'You can believe it if you want but no one survives an explosion like that,' said Mark.

'Lads, start bedding down for the night. If you're staying awake, keep the chat quiet. Heads inside the bags, I don't want ye with pneumonia on the plane to the Leb. Anyone up for a wee during the night, keep the fire going and don't disturb the others. Some of us need our beauty sleep. We'll be on the move after seven, just when it's bright. We are probably three to three and a half hours from camp.'

The next morning was joyous. The fog cleared and, better still, the brightest of the stars were still visible in a navy sky. The sleeping bags had done the trick, given that a white frost was glistening on the mossy stones of the circle. Yet people were reporting that they had slept well. Somebody had been decent, not only getting the fire rekindled but also going to the nearby stream and rinsing out the cups. A mug of milky Joe with a cellophane-wrapped chocolate bread roll would provide just the right energy injection to start the day.

Seeing Martha stretch out her arms as she emerged from the sleeping bag gave Pete the shunt he needed to address the platoon. 'Listen, guys, we're moving out in twenty minutes. We have two choices. Either tell all or tell nothing. But one thing is for sure: if we tell all, there's no plane taking off to the Leb, or at least if there is, we won't be on it.'

The significance of this information started to dawn on the youngsters. Even after yesterday, the excitement generated by the pending trip to foreign lands hadn't evaporated.

'Will those rangers not beat the truth out of us anyway?' asked Jake.

This time Mark answered. He wanted the trip as well, and there was no need, he felt, for Pete to be doing all the talking. 'No. You won't see those guys today. If they don't get you on the first attempt, they don't go a second time. Badge of honour and all that crap.'

While there were murmurs of conversation among the guys, Paul, now steadier than the previous night, made the killer pitch. 'Listen, I'm the clown that nearly did for myself and for others' – He threw a glace at Fionn first and then Martha – 'I'm the one that has to march back into camp with a plastic bag for a boot. I'm on that plane.'

For whatever reason it was the older guys who were secretly relieved. Seamus finished the narrative: 'So one simple story: nothing happened, full stop.'

They trekked on in a line now. The battle-formation diagonal was abandoned, at least until they were in view of the barracks. Peter had wanted to talk with Fionn, just as he had done with Martha the previous night. He was probably using the excuse of Joe's constant presence to avoid the conversation. Anyway, he had eavesdropped in on Fionn's account. His act of bravery had left Peter feeling that sensation in his stomach that came when an opportunity had presented itself and been missed. He had let a kid call it. But more had been gained than lost.

There was a pleasantness to the trek back to Camp Imaal. The weather, the mood, the bond, the agreement. Maybe not quite snatching victory from the jaws of defeat, but at least getting another day for the fight.

Chapter **Five**

The first glimpse the lads got of their new landscape was from the charter as it gradually descended from 36,000 feet. From the chatter, it seemed they had been expecting something out of *Lawrence of Arabia* – rolling sand dunes for as far as the eye could see. The desert would be a novel sight for them, particularly for the lads from the northside of Dublin. Some of them had never strayed south of the River Liffey, never mind the south of the Mediterranean.

But their hopes of seeing miles and miles of undulating sand dunes were immediately dashed. Instead they looked down on a mountain range, rock rather than sand, red rather than yellow. You could already appreciate the oppressive heat in the absence of green in a landscape that could only have been forged under a baking sun.

The plane gave a sudden violent jump, as though it was thumped ten feet upwards.

'Are we after clipping one of those mountains?' asked Private Taylor.

Sergeant Doyle rolled his eyes. 'Soldier, if we clipped one of them hills, I can assure you, me boy, we'd be well on our way to Heaven by now.'

They finally came to a complete stop on a remote concrete runway surrounded by rocky undulating desert, the mountains now in the distance behind them. It had the look of a military installation, judging by the few small, camouflaged buildings that made up the site. The desert air introduced the boys to a different smell. A fragrant, warm smell, which left the impression that something pleasant must grow here during some part of the year. They walked down the aircraft steps and on towards a minibus, which was now approaching the group.

'Me first look at the Leb,' said Taylor.

'I think not, since we're in Jordan,' Sergeant O'Brien replied.

'What, the model?'

'No, Jordan the country, you eejit. Now pipe down, we're off to briefing and billeting. Time for some real soldiering.'

The troop journeyed for about fifty minutes to what was to be home for the next three weeks. They murmured away about the strangeness of not being in the destination they had expected. A lot of them had researched Camp Shamrock in the Lebanon, where to go on leave and all that. This destination, when they arrived, was a stark, fenced-off site. Its eight stone-built single-storey buildings had the grim look of standard military dormitories. The lads were quickly marshalled into one of the buildings, which was set up for briefing purposes.

'Hello, my name is Captain Mohammad Almadi.

On behalf of the Jordanian Army and at the request of the Palestinian Authority, you are all welcome to my country.'

Captain Almadi was the first foreign soldier the young lads had ever encountered and was a relaxed, pristinely dressed officer. He displayed an impressive set of decorations on his uniform. There were a lot of them for a youngish-looking man.

'As United Nations peacekeepers you are mandated under UN resolution 1580 to conduct an observatory mission on sites within the Palestinian West Bank. Your leadership team, Sergeants O'Brien and Doyle, will brief you on your orders. You will be orientating in my country for twenty-one days. Transportation across the Dead Sea has been arranged. I wish you every success in your mission. Inshallah. I will be your platoon liaison for the duration of your stay in Jordan.' He saluted before he left, and everyone rose to give their formal salute.

The sergeants were quietly pleased.

O'Brien thought, At least we've taught them that military is a strong, rigid family. You must have respect, or you have nothing. 'Short and sweet. Gentlemen and lady,' he bellowed, stressing *gentlemen* and de-stressing *lady*, 'all enlisted men will proceed to building four and pick a bunk. Private Martha O'Dowd will bed down in building six. That's your first taste of Islam, Private O'Dowd. No males and females together unless you're married.'

Sergeant Doyle pitched in to hold up his part of

the double act: 'Initial patrol of the terrain in thirty minutes. You'll be covering twenty kilometres. Get your bags from the bus and move it, move it!'

Easy for Sergeant Doyle to say; he was staying behind to mind privates Paul Devitt and Martha O'Dowd while they did barrack sentry duty. Both sergeants had been mildly put out by the change in these two since the last days of basic training. The privates had been quiet and withdrawn and had asked permission to miss the famous end-of-basic-training party in the officers' mess. Nonetheless this was the army, and Sergeant Doyle believed a twenty-four-hour sentry shift in the glaring sun would be just the job for them. That would shake them out of their homesickness or whatever else ailed them.

Sergeant O'Brien had been well briefed on the terrain and was happy to lead the reduced platoon on what, for them, should be a straightforward tour of the surrounding dry country. He had done it in the Lebanon, and this wasn't much different. Both sergeants knew that they would eventually have to field questions about their location and the mission. This was a completely new location for the Irish Army. Even so, the West Bank was, in their opinion, no more volatile than the Lebanon had been when they were there twenty years previously. The youngsters might be oblivious to the situation, but those older privates were likely to be trouble, O'Brien thought. They watched the news. It wasn't lost on the sergeants that this was quite an honour, in a way, to be picked for a new type of mission. This was probably a career swan song for both of them. But again, there was a nagging question: why send a bunch of raw recruits with a couple of briar-like older privates?

Sergeant O'Brien marched off into the afternoon sun with the gang of nine, full packs on their backs and in assault formation to boot. This was the desert winter sun but it was still darned hot. Sergeant O'Brien literally had his satnav up his sleeve. He used a compass and map, in fairness, as a double check. The platoon knew they would not have radio contact with their new base. Leaving within the hour hadn't left time to set up a communications station.

It was less than two weeks since the infamous Wicklow hike, and the youngsters at least were up for a bit of physical exercise. People were feeling a bit rough after a long flight. A bit of exercise would be a welcome relief. O'Brien had the sense to place the older men, Mark and Seamus, at the opposite ends of the diagonal, with him in the middle. This was the sergeant's design so that he wouldn't get an earful of questions from those two. Standard instruction was to only speak to the soldier on either shoulder, and, in a low voice, pass messages along the line. As it turned out, he had Peter and Joe on his immediate right and left.

The trek wasn't long underway when footwear, just like in Wicklow, became an issue. The army didn't seem to do breathable boots, and the soldiers didn't have the cop-on to wear light cotton socks. The lads hadn't a clue about Jordan, but in a way that didn't matter, and for two reasons. One was that they had all thought they would end up in dessert terrain, albeit with more sand than the hard-on-the feet rock they got. Desert they were certainly in, so what did the country's name matter? Secondly, after two and a half hours out, foot blisters were beginning to mean that they didn't care where they were.

Another thing that always caught the Paddies out when they travelled south was how quickly and early darkness falls. Sergeant O'Brien got an uneasy feeling when he copped that the sun was starting to dip. He convinced himself that they could still get to within a kilometre or two of the camp before dark – even more impressive to approach the joint Irish and Jordanian sentries in darkness on his first foot patrol.

Seamus, from the top of the diagonal, filtered word down to the sergeant that there was contact three kilometres due north-east, meaning they were not alone in the desert. In fairness to O'Brien, he immediately replied up the line to change direction and engage with the 'target'. In other words, he wasn't returning to camp and reporting that on the first sighting of inhabitants he decided to keep moving in the opposite direction.

Now Sergeant O'Brien was wishing again he had his choice of corporal with him, someone to confide in and bounce a few ideas off. Fuck it, he thought, it wouldn't have bothered me if we didn't run into anybody today.

It took the platoon about thirty-five minutes to

move into proximity that revealed what the 'target' was.

'Wow, this is the real deal,' Joe murmured when four camels came into view. 'This must be those Bedouin guys.' Maybe a Leaving Certificate geography flashback was kicking in.

The lads' nerves started to abate and fingers disengaged from triggers. Sergeant O'Brien had never ordered them to engage in the first place.

There was a single tent, big enough to walk into without stooping. Strangely, a good fire was burning outside. The only person they could see was a man, as determined by his bulk. The figure was wearing light-blue and grey robes, which shielded his entire body. Only his eyes were exposed through his shemagh.

He began to approach the group of ten soldiers, and when he was close enough, he addressed the man in the centre to show respect, either because he was talking to a senior man, or perhaps because he was talking to the man wearing stripes. The conversation, in what Sergeant O'Brien deemed to be Arabic, was never going to go far.

'I take it none of our number has a word of Arabic,' said O'Brien, addressing his troops but keeping eye contact with the azure blue eyes of the Arab speaker.

'If we had it would make no difference,' Fionn said. 'He's speaking Aramaic. It's a more ancient language.'

On hearing Fionn, the tribesman immediately shifted his gaze towards him.

Removing the covering from his mouth, a torrent

of words sprang forth, as if he thought Fionn might understand. It was at least clear that the desert camper had some issue that warranted urgent attention. When he saw that his words were not understood, he resorted to an equivalent torrent of hand gestures.

'Sarge, I don't speak the language of mad waving hands, but I think you and Fionn are being invited into the tent,' Taylor said.

'Steady now, lads. I don't want to do anything stupid,' Sergeant O'Brien replied.

Fionn broke his gaze from the tribesman to look at O'Brien. Out of the corner of his eye, the sergeant could see Fionn's vivid expression and knew it could be easily interpreted to mean, 'Stop being a fuckin' eejit, Sarge.'

Certainly the Bedouin interpreted it that way, and it resulted in further gestures and entreaties to enter the tent.

Once Fionn took a step forward, Sergeant O'Brien had no choice but to follow suit. They entered an aroma-filled home, where their eyes took a couple of moments to adjust to the darkness. The coolness of the tent was immediately disarming, as was its comfort and spaciousness. The Bedouin was silent now, as if he himself had entered a lair where he did not exert control. The two Irish soldiers became aware of a sobbing sound. A slender figure had its back to them and was rocking gently back and forth over a little child. The woman was robed as heavily as the man, but all in black. The men could only see the face and two small feet at either side of the swaying woman. What they could see looked lifeless and sick. Fionn went into the gesturing business himself and started a conversation with the Bedouin to ask if he had permission to approach the child. The man responded by placing a firm hand upon the woman's shoulder and speaking softly. The result was instant. The woman rose and moved to the far end of the tent. Even less of her face was visible, and although they did not make eye contact, Sergeant O'Brien saw the bloodshot and weary eyes of a young woman.

The man motioned Fionn to move forward, which he did slowly, out of a growing respect for the gravity of the situation. The child was soaking and sick. A plump little girl, maybe less than two years of age. She had the kind of pudginess that a mother would love, knowing it would burn away as soon as the child mastered walking.

'What do you think, Sarge?'

'I think I wish Sergeant Doyle was here instead of me. He was a medical two-striper once upon a time. Look, Private, we must be aware of where we are. I have a responsibility for my men. I'm going to give the order to move out. We will be walking two hours in darkness even if we leave now. We'll report the situation to the Jordanians when we get back.'

The effect of this conversation on the Bedouin couple was immediate. The man started talking and the woman started to cry again, and this time it was audible to the boys outside.

'Sarge, the reason they're making a fuss is because they know their child is close to death. I'm guessing they are part of a bigger group and have been left to catch up when they either bury their little girl or return when she has recovered. They probably think we were sent from God as the girl's last hope. What we must look like, a bunch of pale Paddies in the Jordanian desert. The Jordanian army will not send a medic to a Bedouin camp. It just won't happen.'

'Jaysus,' replied the sergeant. 'What ever happened to an army where soldiers took orders?'

O'Brien was a father himself and somewhere deep down he knew that his private was trying to save him from a memory that might haunt him later. 'For fuck's sake, you that knows it all, what do you suggest?'

'Give me a few minutes,' was Fionn's calm response. He got up and walked out of the tent to find the troops happily sitting around the fire now that there was no heat left in the sun. They had lost no time in taking their boots and socks off.

'Taylor, my man, did I hear you say your ma stocks up with antibiotics when she's in the Canaries?'

'Yeah. So?'

'So I want the answer to my next question to be yes.' Fionn was keeping the situation light-hearted. 'Did you bring any of the ma's drug haul with you?'

'Well yeah, but–'

'Shush, shush.' Fionn stopped Taylor in his tracks. 'I want the answer to my final question to be yes, also. Do you have any on ye now?'

'I do, yeah,' said Taylor as he produced a slightly crumpled white and blue box from the backpack that he had been resting on.

Fionn took a quick look and said, 'Does your mother have life insurance on you, Taylor?'

'What d'ye mean?' replied Taylor, a little miffed to be relieved of his drugs.

'Only fourteen months past their expiry date,' Fionn revealed.

'Well, she only goes to the Canaries every second year.'

'They'll have to do,' said Fionn.

'D'ye mean? You're taking them?'

'Listen, there's a sick child in there whose need is greater, believe me.'

'But what about it if I get sick? You know it's sixty bucks back home for a doctor's prescription. Imagine how much it is here! Yous had better be doing a whip round for me if I get a bad chest or something.'

'Good luck with that,' said Fionn as he went back inside the tent.

Sergeant O'Brien was keeping a useless vigil over the situation.

'Sarge, I think these might be the man for the job,' said Fionn as he popped two capsules from the blister pack.

'Jaysus, Fionn, if that child dies after us giving her medication, we might be fired out of Jordan quicker than planned.'

'It's your call, Sarge, but I wouldn't make the call thinking that we'll be in trouble with Jordanian officialdom. I doubt if they give a tinker's curse for wandering tribesmen.'

'Look at the size of those bloody tablets! A horse would have trouble swallowing them, and that poor little thing is unconscious.'

'Sarge, get himself to get herself over here and paying heed. He'll listen to you.'

When Fionn had their attention, he proceeded with a manoeuvre that he could have anticipated would earn him a blow to the back of the head with a blunt instrument. He rolled the child gently onto her side and popped two of the antibiotic tablets into his own mouth, where the generation of spittle was clearly audible.

Fionn then took a dripping capsule from his mouth and inserted it as a suppository. His actions were more of a surprise to Sergeant O'Brien that the parents, who had implored the pale men for help. The couple probably felt compelled to comply with the Arab tradition of, having asked for alms, accepting what was then offered. Fionn then added a second spittle-lubricated suppository, with the mother drawing a breath in anguish as a weak squeal emanated from the baby. Fionn then produced a notepad, tore out a page and drew a kind of diagram showing sunrise and a sunset. Beside each he placed a capsule that he had burst out of the pack.

'Sarge, you're good at the comms. Explain the plot line, will ye? Remember, just one tablet at a time from now on.'

O'Brien was impressed with his private and hopeful for the child, so he obliged, mumbling, 'I thought I gave the orders round here.' He felt the better for making a decent stab of saving the youngster, even if he realised that Fionn had manoeuvred him into it.

Before they left the tent, Fionn did something that further surprised the sergeant. He placed his hands on the hands of the women and said, 'Talitha, kum, your child will be well.'

O'Brien was surprised both that he would touch the Bedouin woman and at the confident assertion, not to mention the foreign words that the woman, at least, seemed to understand.

The two men now emerged from the tent to be pleasantly warmed by the glow of the fire against a now dark sky.

'Listen up, boys,' Sergeant O'Brien said. 'There's a really sick child in there, so let's keep the noise down. We'll bed down here for the night and move out at daybreak.'

There were a few moans and groans.

'If you could survive a winter's night in the wilds of Wicklow, then a balmy night in the warm desert should be no bother to ye. We'll move a bit away and build our own fire with a bit of kindling from theirs.'

'Sentries will be Pete, Seamus and Joe, in two-hour shifts. If a snake gets into camp on your shift, then you're on the next flight home.'

'Snakes? Who said anything about snakes?' Jake asked.

'I might be needing those feckin' tablets for myself yet,' said Taylor.

When the story of the sick child filtered through the troops, there was a feel-good atmosphere among them. They were part of making a difference instead of just feeling like green donkeys.

But Sergeant O'Brien warned the lads: 'There is a distinct possibility that the little girl might be gone in the morning.'

'Gone where?' asked Jake.

'Dead,' was the sombre reply.

That soured the atmosphere a bit. Still, people were feeling a bit more relaxed as they got their bedding ready and looked forward to a tinned meal heated by the fire.

'Do you think they'll be looking for us back at camp?' asked Jake, probably trying to supress a bit of homesickness.

'Lads, this is an acclimatisation hike. If we can't manage this, it won't be looking good when we land in Palestine,' the sergeant answered. 'We've no radio set-up, but I'll text our situation in to Sergeant Doyle. He'll get it eventually if the signal gets strong during the night. Besides, now that we have a quiet moment, we might return to your adventures in Wicklow that time. You know the rangers reported hearing a detonation from the far side of their position on the mountain at 4.56 p.m.? These things don't go unnoticed.'

Pete quickly intervened before one of the youngsters had a chance to land them in it. 'Wouldn't know anything about that, Sarge.'

Taylor piped up next, either to further distract the direction of the conversation or maybe because he wasn't following the storyline. 'Isn't that some class of sky up there, way better than you would see at home? Jeepers look at the speed of that thing there.' He was pointing at a moving object in the clearest view of the Milky Way any of them had ever had.

'Wow! If that was the star the wise men followed, their bleedin' camels must have been turbo charged.'

'That's the space station, my friend. I don't think it was around two thousand years ago,' replied the sergeant.

They bantered away talking about everything except Wicklow while they munched through their rations. Some of the lads eventually started to drift off to sleep to the noise of what sounded like prayer coming from the tent.

The night passed uneventfully. The sentries kept themselves awake by keeping the small fire going and drinking coffee heated from the meagre flames. They availed themselves of a turf-like material that had been lying beside the Bedouin fire. It was in fact dried camel dung if truth be told. The coffee did take on a peculiar odour.

The next morning in the desert was nearly as crisply chilly as the one two weeks previously in the Wicklow hills, but perfectly dry. The lads were only coming around when the Arab woman emerged from the tent and approached Fionn's sleeping bag. She was carrying a hot drink, judging by the rising steam, and she knelt down to hand it to him. She was calmer than the previous day and in control of her emotions, or at least not crying.

'Inshallah,' she said and touched Fionn's hand.

The man then emerged from the dwelling. He was carrying the still-naked child, whose eyes were now open and looking around, albeit weakly.

'Inshallah,' he said in a tone that seemed to be by way of thanks.

Fionn took in the moment and sipped his jasmine tea.

'They say that word a lot, don't you think? Inshallah,' said Taylor.

'No different from what our grandparents used to say,' Fionn replied. 'God willing.'

The rest of the camp came to life in order to decamp within twenty minutes. The lads left the Bedouin couple in their tent to do what they must, tend to their child. The troops got a further gee up as they approached their own camp some three hours later. The Jordanian guards all applauded the returning platoon. There was no reason to assume that this was to signal anything other than a well done. Perhaps for having the cojones to spend their very first night in the desert, in the desert.

The guys got plenty more exposure to the desert in the following weeks. The platoon went out on acclimatisation hikes every second day. They were tough going but boring to the extent that nothing much, other than foot blisters, happened.

Sergeant Doyle, Martha and Paul had missed out on that first overnight adventure. Maybe, in the storytelling of the future, they would solve that by reinventing a narrative that included them.

Doyle later led the platoon on a hike to the exact coordinates of the Bedouin tent. Nothing remained. The shifting sands had covered everything. The story that the lads discussed around the barracks fire that night had two trains of thought. The pessimistic one was that they were at the wrong location and there was no way the sand could have covered over an encampment.

'Sure, wouldn't there be camel dung all over the place?'

The optimists were happy that it must have been a good ending and that the family had packed up the encampment and moved on.

The Jordanian soldiers who occupied the barracks were, in the words of the Irish, no craic. The green platoon had arrived thinking that they were landing in the Lebanon. There were a lot of tall tales about previous tours in the Leb. There, at least, you could get a bit of downtime in some taverna or other. The Irish were always looking for a drink. In Jordan there was no place to go. Just miles and miles of bleakness, it seemed.

The sergeants held a few mission-briefing sessions with the team and Captain Almadi. But there wasn't a lot of information to be gleaned from them. It had been a novelty to hear that the platoon's destination was Bethlehem. What the Irish soldiers knew about the town was from old Bible stories and new Christmas cards. The task there was described as being to observe and report back. The youngsters didn't quite know what that entailed but it didn't sound too difficult. All the trekking and acclimatisation hikes would have led anyone to believe that the plan was to walk into Bethlehem. It wasn't, but if that's what it came down to, then the boys sure were ready for it. There wasn't any room left on their feet for new blisters to form.

Pete had wanted to use a bit of the downtime to get more out of Fionn about Wicklow. But Fionn always deflected the conversation by saying that the agreement had been to stay shtum about the incident. Walls had ears and all that.

At the very end of their stay in Jordan, there was something of a stir in the barracks when a sizeable caravan of tribal Arabs was sighted approaching the army camp from the north. They were greeted at the gate by the Jordanian sentries, who seemed to be able to manage a discourse well enough. Ultimately the exchange ended with several skins of offering being unloaded at the gate. Sergeant Doyle was summoned by a sentry. He approached Captain Almadi en route.

'Sergeant, what is it your men get up to in this desert of ours? Highly unusual to be offered alms by the Bedouins. Normally they are trying to relieve you of something. Food and drink as an offering of thanks. I'm told that Bedouin fare is very good, but I myself have never tasted it.'

'Well, now is your chance,' the sergeant replied.

'I think not. A gift offered should be for the recipient only. Enjoy and goodbye. Also, good luck with your departure tomorrow.'

There must have been some sort of bad blood between official Jordan and the tribesmen. There was no question of them being allowed onto the military base to deliver their gift. However, the considerable consignment of food and drink would only be handed over when they were allowed meet the 'pale greens' and the 'holy man'.

Captain Almadi was happy enough to allow the meeting to take place at the front entrance to the garrison compound. When the 'green men' emerged, they were reverentially greeted by the group of three riders who had ridden out with the gifts from a bigger group.

Fionn and Sergeant O'Brien were interested to see if they recognised the Bedouin man from that strange night in the desert. It was a joyous occasion in the sense that the visit now confirmed that the sick child of three weeks previously must now be well. They did not see the man, however, and O'Brien wasn't sure he would even recognise him.

The strangeness of the encounter was emphasised when the delegation all bowed to Fionn in unison and then knelt before him to touch his hand. The rest of the Irish lads didn't know what to make of it, and the Jordanians were aghast.

Fionn looked embarrassed and tried, through hand gestures, to transfer whatever credit was due onto Sergeant O'Brien. The Irish boys, always thinking of their bellies, were meanwhile getting a sniff of the aromatic fare. The excuse for a party looked like it would make up for some of the boring nights spent in a barren military outpost.

Larry, Michael and Paul made a fire outdoors for effect. Meals like these were meant to be consumed under the sky. The Jordanians paid no mind to the goings on of the 'mad Irish'. What group of soldiers would be allowed go on the lash the night before a mission?

The Irish sergeants could sense a bit of antipathy from Captain Almadi and his subordinates. They weren't going to buckle and give in to the censure. Instead there was a little bit of payback in their attitude.

'We'll say what our boys and girl are allowed do and we won't be told otherwise.' That included the awkwardness of consuming alcohol in a Muslim country. 'But, sure, how were we to know what was in those skins?'

Spicy, minty meat dishes were wrapped in succulent green leaves, 'and the drink would blow the skull off ye,' Taylor said appreciatively.

It tasted for all the world like a cross between wine and sherry, but not unpleasant.

'Now, lads, eat up,' Sergeant O'Brien said. 'This

is the best return ever for a packet of out-of-date antibiotics. More to the point, that lamb will give you an iron stomach for the crossing tomorrow.'

'Fionn, can I ask ye what do you think we should expect when we make the crossing?' asked a serious Jake. The alcohol was making him more uptight, not less.

'The crossing will be smooth. There won't be even a ripple on that patch of water in this good brisk weather,' Fionn replied. 'I'll say this about the Bethlehem we will find: I don't think it's what Jesus would have expected two thousand years on.'

'Oh, oh, I think we're in for another lecture,' said Taylor.

'No, no,' Fionn said. 'I just think what we'll see in Bethlehem might be a poorer version of what we see at home, as we approach Christmas.'

'Yeah, what's wrong with that? We all get presents, like,' said Taylor.

'Sure, sounds good,' replied Fionn. 'But the volume, the values, the pressure, the anticipation, the stress, the build-up. I don't think this is what makes for a celebration of Jesus, to be honest.'

'Ah bah humbug to ye,' replied Taylor, getting more jovial by the sip.

'At least you can't knock those Bedouin guys,' said Paul, getting into the conversation.

'No, you're right. They have a code that's brilliantly built into their DNA. You reward the kindness and the efforts of strangers,' said Fionn.

'This lamb is lovely,' said Jake, inadvertently changing the subject.

'Ah, all this Christmas talk has you thinking of shepherds and sheep in this part of the world. The Bedouins are goat herders and I'm betting that's what you're eating,' said Fionn.

'Nice anyway, whatever it is,' said Jake.

'Yeah, just like Ma used to make … not. This meal is tasty,' said Taylor.

'No slagging your ma,' said Joe. 'Remember, her tablets were the reason we got this feast.'

Larry got Paul going about his army background. 'Sarges, did you know our Paul knows a lot about the army from his old man and he told us a bit about the Congo.'

'What or where is the Congo?' asked Taylor.

'I think it's called Democratic Republic of Congo these days, in central Africa.'

'The Congo is way back, Paul. Your dad wouldn't be that old?' said Sergeant O'Brien.

'No, Sarge, it was the granda who saw the Congo. Me dad got to make sergeant and did his UN stint in the seventies, in Cyprus of all places. The Turks and the Greeks were replaying ancient history and had their own private war there. That had its excitement, but his old man, my grandfather – another Paul, surprise, surprise – had an even better collection of stories to tell about his time in Africa.'

'Jeepers, quite the military family you guys are,' said Sergeant Doyle.

'The three Pauls. You've a lot to live up to,' said Sergeant O'Brien.

'The grandad, he's dead a good few years now, was in the famous 1950s Battle of the Tunnel. It's famous for a few things. Firstly, it's the only example of a military engagement that the Irish Army won. They lost a few in the Congo as well.'

'What, battles?' asked Michael.

'Battles and men, unfortunately,' answered Paul.

'That's the second thing the battle was famous for: two Irish guys were killed, including a lieutenant. The grandad was really proud of playing his part and was forever showing his pewter mug with a bullet hole in it. Like he said – life-and-death soldiering.'

'Look, lads, you'll have your own service stories in short enough time. Let's make sure we work together so that all the tales we get to tell in the future end happily,' said Sergeant Doyle.

When Larry saw the sergeants head off to presumably take a wee, he lowered his voice. It was still only just a month since Imaal. 'Paul, are you fully the better of your exploits in Wicklow?'

'Jesus, yeah, even more so because Martha and Fionn got the brunt of it, and by the look of them, they're well ready for tomorrow,' replied Paul.

'What would your old man make of it all?' asked Michael.

'You mean if I ever tell him,' replied Paul. 'I really don't know what he'd say, apart from commenting on my own stupidity. But the rest of it ... could we ever tell anyone? Unbelievable stuff, isn't it?'

'Could Martha have imagined it? It was, when you think of it, hugely stressful. I mean … on your knees with a feckin' bomb staring you in the face.'

'I'd say unbelievable is the word for it, all right,' said Larry.

The sergeants came back, keeping their usual distance from the boys but listening in all the same.

'I can't help thinking it was more than the tablets though,' O'Brien said to Doyle. 'We thought Fionn was doing something clever, but the Bedouin couple thought something else was going on.'

'Well, not to worry, if it was divine intervention they were looking for and they feel they got it, what harm?' said Doyle.

'Fair enough, but you did your medical training, would you have come up with a better solution?' asked O'Brien.

Doyle thought about his answer for a second. 'No, I guess if I had been the medic there, the poor child would have died. Look, I'm being a bit flippant. Maybe this drop of drink is stronger than ye think. Fionn is a class act as a young soldier and I'm glad to have him in the boat tomorrow. I just don't want to get carried away with strange ideas, especially on the night before the mission.'

'But we should acknowledge the reverence the young man was shown by a tribe of hardened Arabs,' O'Brien said.

'For sure, and he has influence over our older privates

as well. I'm suspicious that something happened on their last training sortie in Wicklow.'

'If you're referring to the reported detonation then you have to give them credit for keeping their mouths shut. The young and the old. I asked them when we were out in the desert, the first night, but I got no change.'

'I think the older guys are realising that Fionn is more likely to get corporal stripes out of this than they are,' said Sergeant Doyle.

'Yeah, but Peter and Seamus are taking it better than Mark. Funny how people create their own reality. Mark is the least likely of the trio to ever get rewarded,' said O'Brien.

'Yeah, for sure. You can be a pain in the arse but convince yourself otherwise. That's the way the world works, I guess,' said Doyle.

'Anyway, give them another half hour and then bed. We're leaving the dorms at 3 a.m.'

'Best of luck tomorrow, Sergeant.'

'Same to you, Sergeant.'

'We're kind of playing in the big league now, trying to sneak by the Israelis,' said O'Brien.

'We'll do it, I'm sure of it,' was Sergeant Doyle's confident reply.

'What we do in Bethlehem and whether it provokes an Israeli response remains to be seen,' said O'Brien.

'Maybe that's the whole idea – provoke a response on the West Bank before Gaza ceases to be a viable place to live,' said Doyle.

'Jesus, when you say it like that I'm left wondering about our poor little undersized platoon,' said O'Brien.

'When I say it like that, I wonder why there isn't an Irish commissioned officer in sight.'

Chapter **Six**

The United Nations observer mission began for real at 3 a.m. Friday morning. This was the first time the platoon had been entitled to don their bright blue berets. They split up into two boats, with a sergeant in each – standard Navy protocol. Simply stated, if one boat gets holed, you still have a fifty percent chance of success. There was an expected touch of nervousness; after all, this was the dead of night. The boats maintained a blackout stance, with low running speed to avoid noise. This was going to be a long, dark night slowly crossing the Dead Sea.

The crews, when they got underway, were nearly arranged according to boundary lines. Most of the Dubs were together, either by accident or design. In the boat with Fionn were the senior Privates Mark and Seamus and the juniors Taylor, Jake and Joe, under Sergeant Doyle. The sergeant wanted the lads chatting quietly, even though the pilot had insisted on silence. Doyle knew a little bit of constructive chat would calm their nerves.

'Sarge, what's with all the cloak and daggers?' Jake asked.

'Well, let's see now, we're in a Jordanian naval vessel. We're landing in a foreign country. We must make our way to a rendezvous in Bethlehem. What could possibly go wrong?'

'I know you're being smart, Sarge, but we're guests of the Palestinians, yeah?'

'Well, I wouldn't quite say guests, more invitees. You see the problem, my young friend, is that when you set foot in the West Bank, it's bloody hard to be sure what country you're in, Palestine or Israel.'

'Why, is there a problem with their satnavs?' Taylor asked.

The sergeant wondered if he was being annoying or just annoyingly stupid. 'It's not that. It's that these Jewish settlements tend to grow up out of the blue,' Sergeant Doyle continued. 'Remember, lads, as well, tensions have been running high ever since the US moved its embassy into Jerusalem. That's why we're on the mission, to assess how badly that move has further irked the Palestinians.'

'Do you know, Sarge, what Trumpy was playing at with that move?' asked Fionn.

'No, Private, but I have the feeling we're about to get a profound explanation. But seriously, I'd say Jewish money, power and influence has always been a big thing in the US political system. That's my simple guess; no doubt yours, Fionn, is more complicated.'

'He is getting them ready for the second coming,' Fionn said.

'Yeah, he's big into sex and women, that fella,' said Taylor. He couldn't help himself.

'I mean the second coming of the risen Christ.'

Sergeant Doyle knew he had to intervene here, if only to get the lads refocused. 'Now, Private, I've been pleased with your input into our little chat so far, so you're not going to spoil that, are you?'

'Look, I'm not sure that Mr Trump believes in anything much, but he sure does know how to play to an audience.'

'So you're saying, Fionn, that the president of the United States is getting the Jewish people ready for another Jesus?' asked the sergeant.

'No, it's more like the fundamentalist Christian lobby he is getting ready, you know the Bible Belt guys. There's way more of them in the US that there are Jews.'

Private Mark had had enough of what he would call 'shite talk'. 'That's the maddest thing I've ever heard,' he said. 'That fellow would wreck your head, Seamus. What d'you think?' Mark was thick and trying to enlist Seamus's support. He'd decided four weeks earlier that none of these kids, and certainly not Fionn, was going to show him up. The tension and cold, now that they were on the water, wasn't helping his mood. Maybe he resented Fionn, thinking he was laying claim to those elusive corporal stripes.

To use one his mother's favourite phrases, Fionn had about as much interest in stripes as the Man on the Moon. He carried on, oblivious to the negative energy: 'I guess we won't get to see it, but there's a huge necropolis just outside one of Jerusalem's walls.'

'What's a necropolis when it's at home?' Seamus

asked calmly, showing he had no intention of joining in on Mark's attack.

'It's a giant cemetery, but the point is that the Jewish people believe it's the first place where the dead will rise again on Judgement Day. Trumpy wants to be seen to promote recognition of the place.'

'Pure shite talk,' said Mark. He had put in his twelve years and he wasn't going to be told anything by anyone junior to him. Maybe it was a chip-on-the-shoulder kind of thing. Certainly, it was skewed thinking, like how could anything these kids had to say have any value? Mark didn't get Taylor's jovial nature. He thought Jake's quietness was a clear sign of homosexuality. He didn't like the bond between Joe and Fionn. But top of his hit list was Fionn's character. Whether it was the fact that Fionn was action-oriented, that he got on and did things, or just that he had demonstrated sound judgement, there was a lot to dislike if your motivation was warped. He felt even the sergeant had to be with him on this one. He surely couldn't let that Fionn guy away with this level of rubbish talk.

Before the tetchiness could escalate further, the cover of darkness was suddenly broken by three massive searchlights. An amplified voice boomed, 'Israeli Army. Cut your engines immediately and prepare to be boarded.'

There was silence on the boat. It took a while for the pilot to realise that all the searchlights were trained on the other boat. He had not been spotted. The address had been aimed at Sergeant O'Brien's vessel. How could this be? The searchlights had strobed them, but the pilot, paralysed by the approaching threat of an Israeli gunboat, had not cut his engine. The boat was now three hundred metres away, receding into the darkness.

Doyle stealthily approached and had a quick, whispered conversation with the pilot. He returned to his men and gave them an update.

'Orders are to keep going if one vessel is detained. I have no control over this, lads. Feck, where's Fionn?'

The soldiers quickly looked around but Fionn was gone.

'He must have slipped into the water, Sarge.'

'We can hardly conduct a search with a gunboat bearing down on all of us, can we?' whispered Mark.

Sergeant Doyle hurried back to the pilot to report the new urgent development. As he knew it would, the plan remained the same. This Jordanian was a man for following orders, particularly if it meant avoiding a beating and probably a prolonged stay in a sweltering Israeli military jail. Onward they went. It wasn't down to Pete this time; now it was Sergeant Doyle's turn to wonder how he would explain losing a man on an observer mission.

Chapter **Seven**

Bethlehem

Sergeant Doyle and his rattled troop approached the shore just as a brightness was appearing in the eastern sky. The original plan had been to land an hour before dawn. Doyle's head was spinning. He knew damn well the unfolding events would define him as a man and as a soldier. How does it get to be so? A whole life soldiering, highs and lows, the comradery, and it all seemed to be unravelling in an instant. It was very likely that Private Fionn O'Toole had drowned in the Dead Sea. Isn't that what that goddamn sea was famous for? Doesn't everything float in it, but nothing survives in it?

Doyle had to keep his hopes up; otherwise he would be no good to his men. But how could he? The sergeant was remembering the clarity of the Jordanian captain's briefings: 'If you try a front crawl in the Dead Sea, the extreme salinity will burn the eyes out of your head. But don't worry, your lungs will have collapsed long before then.'

An inflatable dinghy with a quiet on-board motor pulled alongside their vessel, about one hundred metres from shore. The Irish troop disembarked. The pilot saluted and was away, conscious he should have been using the cover of darkness to return to Jordan. But time had been lost drifting quietly away from the pillars of light from the Israeli frigate's searchlights. Still, none of them knew how they had evaded detection. The pilot had shared with Sergeant Doyle his fear that they would be tracked, cat and mouse, all the way to shore. It seemed not.

A contingent of three, including a short, barrel-chested man complete with impressive moustache, met the Irish soldiers on the beach.

'I am Ibrahim, Mayor of Bethlehem. Ahlan wa sahlan. On behalf of the elected administration of the occupied territory of Palestine, I welcome you. It is imperative that we leave quickly, as soon as the second vessel arrives.'

What Ibrahim said next was so bizarre that it shook an already shaken Sergeant Doyle.

'Where is the Holy Man, Fionn? He is with the other boat, yes?'

'Mayor, I regret to inform you that Private Fionn O'Toole was lost overboard during our contact with an Israeli gunboat. Our second vessel was detained.'

'That is a great loss. Allah will mourn such a loss. Fionn has been making a great stir of news. Inshallah, I will explain all, but we will proceed with haste to the sacred place of Bethlehem, as planned, albeit with half our honoured peacekeeping force.'

The two bodyguard types accompanying Ibrahim quickly encouraged the party into an anonymous-looking twenty-seater white van.

On the drive to Bethlehem the men could see the breaking dawn through the vehicle's skylights; the side windows were blacked out. Joe more than any of them was in a state of shock. He was looking up at something they had all seen that night in the Jordanian Desert: the International Space Station. Its beacon-like sharp spot of light overtook them directly overhead. Could his best buddy be dead in the toxic cold water of a Dead Sea? The thought of Fionn's mother being left all alone, the only light of her life gone and gone for ever, was killing him.

Everyone was mostly silent for the forty-minute journey. Even the Palestinian delegation were quiet. Sergeant Doyle didn't know if this was out of respect for their loss or because of anxiety about the territory they were journeying through. There were signs, surprisingly in English: YOU ARE USING THIS ROAD AT YOUR OWN RISK.

The majesty of arriving into Bethlehem was lost on the silent group. The drive had taken less than an hour on a surprisingly good road. Chosen, no doubt, to avoid any Israeli intervention. The final two kilometres were a descent from the hills into a mist-covered town. It was early Friday morning and the place showed no signs of coming to life. It struck Sergeant Doyle that the mist was affording the town a kindness by disguising a decay in the low-rise dwellings that he could glimpse through the windscreen.

Step one, just the same as it was in Jordan and

just the same as it was in all military operations, the debriefing while everything was still fresh in your head. Sergeant Doyle composed himself. They had pulled into the courtyard of a compound of two-storey buildings. The structures were new but trying to look old world, classic sandstone architecture of the Middle East. The render finish was the pale-yellow of the surrounding terrain, the buildings and the desert.

Unlike in Jordan, this debriefing was to be conducted by men in suits, of which there were three. Mayor Ibrahim introduced them to what seemed to Doyle to be a very up-beat Palestinian group. The mayor, having been seated, stood up and placed himself behind the two other seated officials. He addressed the standing Sergeant Doyle and his five soldiers.

'As-salaam alaikum. You are most welcome guests of the Palestinian people and we recognise your official United Nations mandate.'

Sergeant Doyle saluted in return, and his troops, all standing, saluted in unison.

'We regret the unfortunate circumstances of your loss, but perhaps all will be for the best, Inshallah.'

'I'm not sure the Irish Army will view the loss of a young soldier as the best situation, Mayor.' The sergeant was understandably tetchy in his response but still used the word *loss* and not *death*.

'Of course, of course,' returned the mayor, aware that he had given offence. 'But perhaps you are unaware of certain developments. There are stories in the print media coming from Dublin. The *Herald* has interview with Mrs Kathleen O'Dowded.'

'Who is she when she's at home?' asked Doyle, a bit too smartly, perhaps, but adrenalin and shock were kicking out and in and making unhappy bedfellows, even for a hardened sergeant.

'Mrs Kathleen O'Dowded claims to be the mother of one of your soldiers, a Private Martha O'Dowded.'

The mayor's English was good, but the Irish names were killing him. The penny dropped for Doyle and for the rest of his boys. They were all fully alert now.

'Apologies, Mayor, please update us as to your intelligence.' The sergeant's tone was more conciliatory.

'In her interview she tells of receiving a letter from the Irish Army to say that her daughter has been dispatched to the Golan Heights in Syria and not the Lebanon as she had been previously informed. This seems to have caused Mrs O'Dowded concern enough to contact the *Herald* with a strange story.'

'When did all this occur?' asked the sergeant.

'Allow me to show you the headline.' The mayor signalled to one of his subordinates at the table, who duly opened out a standard A3 sheet, which contained a scan of the newspaper's front page. The man oriented the page so that Sergeant Doyle and the rest of his men could draw round and see it for themselves: MOTHER CLAIMS SOLDIER DAUGHTER PUT IN FURTHER DANGER AFTER BEING BLOWN UP.

'Quite a headline, you think, yes?'

'Mayor, when you picked us up, you knew one of my soldiers by name – Fionn,' Doyle said.

'Yes, indeed, Flonn the holy,' replied the mayor. 'Perhaps I can summarise. Mrs Kathleen O'Dowded is saying her daughter was blown up by a bomb during her training. She says her nerves could not take the strain of the letter from the Irish Army. It stated her daughter was not gone to the relative safety of the Lebanon but was in fact dispatched to the Golan Heights. This you know to be in Syria. Quite a geography lesson. One where perhaps your military were trying to be too clever in not revealing the true location of your mission. For obvious reasons. Better still, she goes on to say her daughter was killed and was brought back to life by her friend Flonn.'

Sergeant Doyle turned his head to look at Private Joe.

No one said a word.

On the Friday afternoon the five Irish privates were forced out on an orientation tour of Bethlehem. The show apparently had to go on. To them it was a surprisingly neglected place that could have done with a bit of upkeep.

Given the situation, they were glad to be welcomed into the Church of the Nativity for a private, arranged visit. The priest blessed them and offered prayers for Fionn. That was consoling. Even so, Joe started crying. The Arab priest took him aside into a private anteroom.

When he gathered himself, Joe asked, 'Would you send a text message to an Irish mobile for me?'

'If it is permitted, I will hand you my phone.'

'Thank you, Father, but my fingers are trembling.'

Dermot and Mary had immediately gone to Fionn's mam's place. Poor Margaret was dazed, unable to take in what was being said.

'My only son, my only son,' she repeated to a crying Mary, who was already embracing her.

'We can't give up all hope,' said Dermot. 'You know the army haven't said anything.

'Dermot,' said his wife, 'don't you think that speaks volumes?'

The Irish boys were celebrities the people of Bethlehem had been expecting, it seemed. The ordinary beleaguered people couldn't be accused of any wrongdoing. They appreciated the young men who were prepared to risk themselves for, as they saw themselves, a downtrodden race. Even contrary Mark enjoyed the bit of stardom. They were heroes, the first United Nations observer mission or intervention since 1967. It was a mission they undertook at considerable risk to themselves, a mission that, it was reported, had already lost these boys a friend and comrade.

The Saint Gabrielle Hotel was the new green base, and the soldiers were afforded their meals for free. No one had an appetite, though. The hotel was an ordinary, clean place for pilgrims, really. The atmosphere was lifted a little by the Advent decorations that had been recently added.

So much for a clandestine observer mission, more like a set-up with me as the fall guy, Sergeant Doyle thought as he observed the choreography around him. He knew the Israelis could do nothing rash to thwart the media attention that the Palestinians would now revel in.

Doyle himself was feeling low. He had to clutch on to something positive, but there was nothing positive about his 'holy soldier' being presumed dead.

Chapter **Eight**

Mrs O'Dowd made her television debut in time for the lunch-time news on Friday. This was a follow-up to her earlier interview with a nice man from the *Evening Herald*. She was prepared to stand on her doorstep while an RTÉ microphone was thrust in the direction of her gob. There was competition for space: the print journalists had been hanging around for pretty much twenty-four hours, by that stage. The path to her front door had an iron railing on one side and a privet hedge on the other, so there was limited space. On the terraced near neighbours' side, the other side of the iron rail, was the Murtaghs' house. The media had encroached on the portly and somewhat irate Harry Murtagh's pathway. 'Get the bloody hell out of me garden or I'll set the dog on ye,' he told the gathered media.

In fairness, the Murtagh family had been virtual prisoners in their own home for the best part of a day. Harry didn't want himself or his clan tackled or photographed by the media. The family had resorted to sending the grandson on missions over their back wall to go to the local shop for bread, milk, cigarettes and the like.

Mr Murtagh was at least hopeful that the media

attention would soon dry up. He based this on the fact that his neighbour and friend Mrs O'Dowd was turning out to be a one-trick pony. Like a good court witness, she didn't vary her story.

'All I'm telling ye is her soldier friend Fionn did a miracle on her after she was blown up.'

Full stop.

The media had taken to breaking the siege every two hours or so. They would take turns knocking at the door to draw our further details of the 'miracle' story. The ever-courteous Mrs O'Dowd would offer very little extra, but she did add a bit of intrigue, because she kept changing the name of the hero. He was, variously, Fintan, Finn or Fionn, depending on her mood.

When she answered her door for the first time in the darkness of the December Friday evening, the intrigue intensified. Firstly because of the glare of the media lights in the darkness, and secondly because the number of microphones had grown significantly. A female reporter with an American accent asked her about reports that her daughter had been captured by the Israeli Army. If that wasn't enough of a cage-rattler, the reporter followed up immediately by asking for a comment on the statement that one of the Irish soldiers was missing, presumed dead. Mrs O'Dowd turned visibly pale and looked for a moment like she might fall backwards as she joined up the concepts of dead and captured.

Mr and Mrs Murtagh emerged from their adjacent

front door. They had been watching through the parlour window and would not leave their friend in distress any longer. Mr Murtagh climbed awkwardly over the metal railing, right leg first so his bum was to the media. When his left leg had cleared the obstacle, the bulky Mr Murtagh took up nearly the entire width of the narrow path. He moved forward, arms outstretched down the path like a snow plough, clearing reporters. A nimbler Mrs Murtagh meanwhile slipped over the railing to embrace her neighbour and prevent her from toppling over.

Commandant O'Mahony had experienced the glare of the media on the Irish Army during his thirty-year career. There had been, for example, a long-running saga concerning the deaths of two privates in the Lebanon in the eighties. That tragedy seemed to resurface every three to four years as the alleged perpetrator went through various stages of a deportation prosecution. On a less serious note, there were also some good news stories around lending a hand during snow storms, bus strikes, refuse-collection mutinies, etc.

O'Mahony had never experienced a media shit storm like this before, though. He would have loved to hide behind the cathedral-like walls of McKee Barracks, but there was no possibility of that. The minister had him virtually holed up in Government Buildings while a legion of suits formulated the best media spin.

But the Irish were behind the black ball on this one. NBC, Fox, Sky, BBC, RTÉ were all in frenzy mode. Some of the Saturday morning soundbites:

'Irish platoon captured in Israel.'

'One soldier missing, presumed drowned.'

'Outrage at no search undertaken for missing Irish soldier.'

'Israeli Ambassador summoned to Department of Foreign Affairs.'

The Irish Army chief of staff together with the minister for defence and the hapless Commandant O'Mahony had been debriefed by Sergeant Kevin Doyle. Doyle was flanked by the Mayor of Bethlehem who had laid on as secure a Skype video link as the Palestinian administration could execute. Doyle took full responsibility for the loss of Private Fionn O'Toole.

When asked about a search and recovery mission, the mayor had been adamant: 'My friends, regrettably the Dead Sea will be a swarm of Israeli naval vessels.'

If that wasn't problematic enough, there was also the matter of six captured Irish military personnel, together with one Jordanian naval pilot. Even the best PR person that the Irish Army or the UN could buy would struggle to spin this situation.

Certainly, the first Irish Army press conference on Saturday afternoon was a disaster. The UN headquarters in New York was a long way from both Dublin and Palestine. It was the weekend, which for New York was as good an excuse as any to say nothing. The message was: hang the Irish out to dry. The Irish government had made the strongest representation for the release of its six detained military personnel, given the difficult circumstances of a missing comrade. The statement was delivered from the steps of the Department of Foreign Affairs. The Department of Defence was ruled out as a venue for two reasons. One was that it was a shabby building outside the city centre. The second reason was that there was known to be a few headcases working in Defence. You couldn't risk some gormless-looking soul skulking around in the background in camera shot.

The normally coherent government press officer was struggling on, trying to make the Army look competent. Credible would be a bonus. Serious matters concerning Irish society often have a nasty habit of descending into farce, and this farce kicked off in spectacular fashion.

No sooner had the press officer stopped talking than the screen switched to Tel Aviv. The caption at the bottom told the viewers that Ben Dannell, a member of the Knesset, was speaking. A single red Fox microphone indicated somebody had an exclusive. Member Dannell looked and sounded about as conciliatory as a bulldog.

He had not been sent to win friends and influence people. Hard-line and all as he came across, the Irish had given him plenty to fan the flames with.

'It would seem that the Irish government is having some difficulty with its counting. We have, in fact, yesterday detained seven Irish military personnel, who I might add were illegally attempting to enter the State of Israel.'

'The Irish Army has admitted that seven personnel were detained including one Jordanian national,' the interviewer contributed.

'I say again, we have lawfully detained seven Irish military. How difficult can it be to count?'

Member Dannell held up his two hands to the camera and in a mocking gesture began to count using his fingers.

The Irish public were outraged that a search of the Dead Sea had not been undertaken. Joe's dad had been foremost in the call for one to take place. Dermot didn't particularly want to stand in front of an RTÉ camera but felt he would do it to represent his friend Margaret's voice. Neither the media nor the army had yet confirmed the name of the missing soldier.

When the Knesset story broke, on Saturday evening, it turned the whole situation on its head. It was a hugely unexpected lift to all after twenty-four hours of despair. The three parents had stayed together in Margaret and Fionn's house on Friday night. They had very little sleep.

The arrests on the Dead Sea had taken place in the early hours of Friday morning. Mr Dannell's interview was repeatedly replayed on Sky News all Saturday evening.

'What the feck is going on?' was Dermot's repeated refrain. It wasn't anger or frustration anymore; now there was hope in him. Dermot would have loved to have been able to contact his boy with the news.

Joe had been better able to come to terms with his feelings by talking to Eleanor over email. He had based himself in the relative calm of an internet alcove in the Saint Gabrielle lobby. Joe was using Eleanor's Gmail replies to soothe his own anguish.

'You know, they cover this in training – losing a comrade and still having to move on, like if you were in a battle. But it's all just shite. When it actually happens, your legs are jelly and your head is a mess.' Joe was typing with his eyes watering. He rubbed them so he could see the screen.

All the lads had been thinking and talking over their bond with Fionn. The 'miracle' story was never meant to be shared outside of the eleven who had been in Imaal. Now it was all over the place. The lads wanted to talk over what was it about Fionn that was different. Like a wake, talking about him dulled the pain of losing him. Taylor was now over-the-top sorry he had made such a song and dance about the antibiotics in the desert. Even Mark was feeling meek. He had made a habit out of baiting Fionn, albeit unsuccessfully. Now the locals were lauding him as a hero and that was kind of down to Fionn.

Joe was emailing Eleanor: 'He wasn't so much a stand-out but a standalone boy, like in the way he would call out bullies in school. But in the army, he's been way more different. He leads, and maybe the sergeants try and disguise their regard for him.

They're probably confused, wondering if he is their missing lieutenant, never mind their missing corporal. But the things he has done. Eleanor, I was there in the Glen in Wicklow. We were still trying to make it out to be a lucky coincidence, surviving the explosion. And he's done other things, maybe not as spectacular, but you should have seen the reverence that a Bedouin tribe showed to a twenty-year-old Irish boy.'

Eleanor replied: 'Joe, I only met him that night in the mess with the wine. That was good all right, but he was very withdrawn after that.'

'Yeah, that's my point. When he does these unusual things, they seem to suck the energy out of him for a while. Then he's grand again, one of the lads, well maybe a better version of one of the lads. I can't believe he's gone, Eleanor.' Joe was glad she couldn't see him crying.

'Is he gone, though?' Eleanor replied.

'Eleanor, I was sitting beside him when the Israeli gunboat searchlights came on us, and then he was gone into the water.'

'No, Joe, that's not what I mean. There's some mad-looking guy on the TV, a politician from Tel Aviv. He's smirking and counting on his fingers. The caption underneath says, "Israeli Naval personnel have detained seven Irish UN soldiers for illegally entering the State of Israel." The maths is wrecking me head. Does that not mean …?'

Joe spoke out loud the words he was typing, not caring who was listening in the hotel lobby. 'Oh God, could it be another Fionn trick?' To Eleanor, he sent: 'I'm going to sign off for now, love. We're not meant to be in contact with home but I'm going to borrow a mobile off Mohammed behind reception and ring or text the aul' fella whether it's allowed or not.'

Sergeant Doyle hadn't been able to openly express himself to his own commanding officer, simply because the Palestinian hosts were always present on the Skype calls. Doyle now saw that the observer mission was always going to fail, and his growing suspicion was that that was what the Palestinians wanted. It was possibly what the United Nations wanted as well. A publicity stunt. If an Irish soldier's death served their agenda, all the better. It dawned on Doyle that the two troops the platoon had split into were never going to reach Bethlehem unscathed. The real mystery was how even one of them had made it at all, travelling through the disputed territory between the Dead Sea and Bethlehem. Doyle could see that strings were being pulled, but he didn't know who the puppet master was.

Joe caught Sergeant Doyle out of the corner of his eye as he entered the hotel lobby. He looked like a man on a mission to round up his soldiers and bring a bit of order before the good people of Palestine got his lads imbibing more than was good for them. Joe approached him.

'Sarge, I need a word. There's some great breaking news.' Joe outlined the recent twist to Doyle. Hardened old army hack or not, a lightness spread over the beleaguered sergeant's face.

'You're sure?' It was as if he was thinking, If Fionn is alive, if Fionn is alive.

Joe let the man gather his thoughts. 'Do ye think the Palestinian boss men have heard the news?'

'Son, they know all right, to be sure. They know more than they're letting on. Now, Private, gather up the lads. I want to stop them drinking and, thank God, brief them on the latest situation or miracle or whatever you want to call it.'

Chapter **Nine**

Jerusalem

The Israelis boarded the captured vessel and wasted no time in terrorising its occupants. The pilot was slammed in the jaw with the butt end of a compact sub-machine gun. Soldiers or not, fear is fear, and in the starkness of the glaring spotlights, Sergeant O'Brien was feeling his men's fear and trying to suppress his own. 'Don't be afraid,' came a voice beside him. O'Brien was further disorientated. Fionn had just spoken. He's not in my troop, is he? O'Brien thought. He was desperately trying to get his thoughts straight in a moment he knew could change things for ever.

The other Irish lads were trying to toughen it out as the Israeli soldiers roughly pushed through them, having demanded that they raise their arms in the air. The Jordanian vessel suddenly had a claustrophobic feel about it. The five-man boarding party meant that there wasn't enough room to swing a cat.

Fionn was the next man to get a rifle butt in the jaw, in recognition of the fact that he had shown no interest in raising his arms at all. Private Larry, the man from Donegal, had been standing beside him, arms compliantly raised. He suddenly brought his forehead down full force on the bridge of the nose of Fionn's assailant – quite a feat given that the Israeli was wearing a combat helmet. Obviously, Larry had completed that manoeuvre before.

The backlash was swift but it wasn't inflicted upon Larry or Fionn but on the Jordanian pilot. Maybe a young Israeli soldier had seen a chance to make a name for himself. In an act of savage retaliation, he smashed the butt of his rifle into the small of the Arab's back. The crack was audible. The pilot's head was now looking up at the sky at an impossible angle given that his body was now draped over the steering wheel of the vessel, with his hands still clutching the wheel.

All was suddenly silent. Martha was the first to drop her hands and move. She pirouetted to the side to vomit aggressively into the sea.

The second person to break the paralysis was Fionn. He removed his hand from his own jaw, revealing a small smattering of blood around his mouth. He went over to the pilot, who was moaning in pain. He moved to the front of the wheel, facing the Jordanian. No one stopped him. He had to throw his leg over the steering column that filled the space between the wheel and the windscreen. Still silence – a human life destroyed, an incident that would inevitably be dismissed as an act of defence. A dismissal might not even be required if the attack didn't generate any media coverage. For the soldier who had committed the crime there would be life-changing consequences of a different kind. He could either toughen it out and justify it to himself as a necessary act of heroism in defence of Israel. Or he could crack and let his demons make him admit that he had made the mistake of his life and ended another.

Fionn, unimpeded, cupped the back of the pilot's head with his left hand and slipped his right hand under the pilot's shirt, seemingly feeling for the wound on the Jordanian's back.

An Israeli captain made eye contact with Sergeant O'Brien. Military men knew instinctively who was in command, irrespective of uniform.

'What is your private trying to do here, Sergeant? Straighten him, is it?'

Maybe the two men had different experiences of the savagery of combat. The sergeant knew he had to respond assertively for the sake of his men.

'Quite probably, Captain, quite probably,' the sergeant replied.

The boat was mostly still, moored to a much larger gunboat, about twice the keel.

Fionn was now effectively hugging the Jordanian pilot whose name he didn't even know. The hug was almost pathetic to look at because of the awkwardness of the steering wheel between the two.

The audience, Jews and Gentiles alike, knew that they wouldn't qualify as human if they couldn't at least acknowledge and permit the comfort of human contact being offered to a wounded soldier. The pilot was now perfectly upright.

Fionn leaned over and whispered in his ear, 'Ahmed, you will walk again.'

The whole scene was static, as if the sea had suspended its gravitational relationship with the moon. Maybe nature's forces were temporarily being used for an alternative purpose.

None of the Israeli soldiers were speaking, neither the boarding party nor the contingent six feet above, who were peering over the side of the frigate.

Fionn's whispered voice and the name Ahmed echoed in the still air.

Ahmed moved slightly. His whisper was just about audible. 'Bring me to Al-Quds in order to give thanks.'

The Israeli captain was the first of the boarding party to react: 'Secure the prisoners on board and make sail for Kalia Beach. It will be getting light. Full speed.'

The troop were encouraged this time, not manhandled, to clamber up the six feet using rope ladders. They managed a recovering Ahmed with a bit of ingenuity. Michael was a big lad who might have spent a bit of time in Tralee rugby club judging from the manoeuvre he managed.

'Peter and Larry, would you scale the rope supporting this man on either side. I'll have me shoulders between his legs, to push him along. He won't fall, but sure don't worry if he does – we'll just get Fionn to do another job on him.'

That's the Irish for you: a near-death experience one minute and cracking a joke the next. Seeing that the Israelis had lost their appetite for smacking anyone else was a bonus. Even Private Martha had recovered sufficiently to utter a few words. She hadn't heard Michael's light-hearted jibe.

'Jaysus, don't drop Ahmed, if that's what his name is, boys, or he'll definitely break his back this time.'

It might have been funny under other circumstances, but no one responded. The lads, and particularly Michael, were struggling with the weight of the plump Jordanian.

Fionn was equally silent and looked like he barely had the energy to hoist himself up the ladder. The Israelis weren't up for helping either.

What amazed Sergeant O'Brien was that the Israeli lads were completely deflated. He thought they would have been relishing the kudos of detaining a United Nations taskforce. And what was this guy Fionn? He certainly was unlike any soldier O'Brien had ever commanded.

The sergeant was the last to board the boat. He was afforded that dignity, at least: the men first, the commander last was the protocol. Addressing the sergeant, the Israeli captain said only, 'You and your men will be interrogated when we reach Jerusalem.' The pilot craft was cut loose and quickly drifted off against a brightening sky.

The early Friday morning for the detained seven was initially not unlike the experience of the six escapees. The gunboat made good time to a beach, where inflatables to get ashore and a fortified transporter awaited. It looked like a standard vehicle for transporting convicts. It seemed strange to Sergeant O'Brien that if his friend and colleague Sergeant Doyle had made it to shore, then he would be travelling, at this time, by road to Bethlehem. As it was, he was on the road to Jerusalem, only thirty kilometres north. What type of country was this, he wondered.

The vehicle had benches on each side, facing each other. There was an internal light on because the narrow-slit windows did not allow for much natural light to enter. The road signage they glimpsed made it clear they were en route to Jerusalem. They also knew they were passing through Palestinian territory because of the massive walls on either side of sections of the motorway. These walls were festooned with any number of inward-looking cameras. Having been ushered through two armed checkpoints, they entered a motorway tunnel.

An amazingly recovered Ahmed broke his silence and spoke as they emerged into the light. 'Al-Quds, Al-Quds.'

There it was in all its early morning glory. The Holy City, with that characteristic golden dome visible above the pale-yellow city walls.

'Jaysus, he's a man of few words anyhow,' said Pete.

'He's saying, "The holy",' said Fionn.

'Yeah, what does that mean, though?' asked Pete

'It's the Arab name for their sacred city of Jerusalem. He just got a glimpse of it through the slit.'

There was a bit of a kerfuffle among the lads as they adjusted themselves to get a squint at their destination. It was magnificent, with signs indicating that they must be passing by the Jewish quarter.

It was the same misty morning that the guys arriving in Bethlehem had experienced. Jerusalem was an Israeli city now. It had looked majestic in the distance and even more so when the transporter passed close enough to read a pedestrian sign for Dung Gate. The city was immaculate, ancient but maintained, loved, nourished and cherished. The shame was that what awaited the captives was interrogation and not the celebratory welcome afforded to their escaped colleagues in Bethlehem.

Old Jerusalem is a square city of walls. Nothing in Jerusalem is expansive. Space is too important. Even the police depot they pulled into had to make do with a smallish square. The courtyard allowed the long-wheel-base vehicle to enter. But the same vehicle could only leave following a three-point turn. Four armed Israeli soldiers flanked the vehicle. O'Brien's men seemed reasonably relaxed, possibly relieved at being over the worst of it. You can't be captured twice, and how bad could interrogation be compared to what they had just been through?

The sergeant was thinking that the tiredness that hits the body after an adrenalin rush was an interrogator's friend. Ahmed stood out as being maybe frightened or agitated, and certainly alert. O'Brien, recognising his discomfort, spoke to him: 'Ahmed, my friend, you're under a UN banner while you're with me. You will be treated as one of us.'

'I think not, Sergeant, I am an Arab. Remember, I should already today be dead except for this Holy Man.'

He nodded towards Fionn. The conversation ended abruptly with the back door of the vehicle being opened. Sergeant O'Brien wondered why the aggressive shouts of the Israeli soldiers were absent now. Maybe they were showing reverence to the city they were in. Ahmed wasn't wondering.

'Grenade!' he shouted, piercing the silence as he violently lurched forward and grabbed the off-balance Israeli soldier who had semi-leaned into the vehicle through the half-open back door. Stunned silence. There was a grunt from Ahmed, born out of the physical effort of hauling a skinny soldier by the scruff of the neck and slapping his face onto the floor of the vehicle.

'Brace yourselves!' screamed Ahmed.

As Sergeant O'Brien scrambled for some kind of cover, he copped that the Arab was holding the side of the Israeli soldier's face down on top of the canister he had tossed into the vehicle.

The explosion was a volcano of noise, flash and smoke. Nobody could see into or out of the vehicle. The shouting from outside the vehicle revealed that the yard was now packed with an attack force.

Sergeant O'Brien knew that whatever had just happened was now a life-or-death situation. That was a stun grenade. Would the next one be a real one? O'Brien seized the moment, clambered over the two bodies lying on the vehicle floor and grabbed at any grip he could feel on the vehicle's back door, slamming it shut.

Even with ears ringing, the boys could hear Ahmed. 'I knew what was coming,' he said. 'Throw a stun grenade into the space and soften them up before interrogation. It is an Israeli dirty trick we know of.'

To Sergeant O'Brien's alarm, Ahmed removed his weight from the Israeli soldier's torso and removed an Uzi sub-machine gun that was strapped across his shoulder.

'Hold on, Ahmed,' said Sergeant O'Brien. 'Let's not do anything rash.'

Meanwhile Fionn had gathered himself and was leaning down to attend to the stricken soldier on the floor. 'Martha, get me that green case on the wall above your head. This man needs aid.'

'First aid?' asked Pete. 'Is he even alive?'

'Yes, thank God,' was Fionn's simple reply.

'Blinded, blinded,' the Israeli soldier said, barely audible.

'What is your name?' Fionn asked him.

'Blinded, blinded. David.'

Fionn motioned Martha to grab the stricken David from one side under the arm, and together they lifted him into a sitting position, still on the floor.

If David was conscious enough to know what was going on, he would have been disconcerted by the gasps from the men when they saw the side of his face through the clearing smoke. It had borne the full force of the stun grenade's explosion. No matter. Fionn and Martha quickly and gently massaged burn ointment on to the soldier's cheek. A semi-conscious, docile, and shocked David allowed Fionn to deal with his damaged right eye. They had found a bottle of saline solution in the first aid pack. He applied that to a clump of cotton wool and did something that only Ahmed appeared to notice – he gently spat on the cotton wool and then delicately pressed it on David's right eye, while Martha fixed it in place with a bandage.

Sergeant O'Brien was more tuned in to what was going on outside while the treatment was going on.

'Do not be worried, Sergeant. God is with us today,' Ahmed said.

O'Brien was less than consoled. Militarily there were two options: a hostage and siege situation, or the van door was about to be blown off and casualties from the ensuing assault would be huge or even total. Certainly, Ahmed would not survive it. Sergeant O'Brien didn't like the look of the situation. There was plenty of roaring and shouting outside and coughing and spluttering inside. This didn't give his head much space for thinking. The fact that Ahmed was holding a loaded Uzi and pointing it at the back door did grab the sergeant's attention, however.

The chain of command had become a bit blurred between Sergeant O'Brien and Ahmed. The fact that Fionn often assumed the lead anyway muddied the waters even further. But in this case, he at least was busy dealing with the afflicted Israeli.

The cleansing and cooling effect of the ointment seemed to comfort David. The amateur medics left him with a clean cotton dressing over his right eye and cheek bone and a matching white bandage around his head to keep the dressings in place.

Fionn's calmness while bathing and cleansing a Jewish soldier must have had a calming effect on the rest of the men. Now that the smoke had dissipated from the vehicle, the situation was becoming clearer. Sergeant O'Brien knew he had a bit of time. It was when the roaring and shouting outside stopped that time would run out. He assessed the situation with his military brain now fully switched on. They were in a robust bomb-proof vehicle with narrow-slit, reinforced-glass windows. They had a naval pilot, Ahmed, with an Uzi sub-machine gun trained on the only entrance to the vehicle. They had an Israeli outfit outside that seemed to be in disarray.

Fionn, assisted by Martha, lifted David into a more comfortable position, onto one of the side benches in the vehicle. While most people had their eyes trained on the back door, Martha saw Fionn bring his mouth close to the stricken soldier's ear.

He whispered, 'Your eye will see again, my friend.'

Martha wasn't sure if the others had heard above the din from outside.

'Ahmed,' said Fionn, 'hand us over that auld machine gun. Sarge, I think we would be better off returning this boy to his rightful owners.'

Sergeant O'Brien's mouth was open.

Uncharacteristically, the words would not come. Even more gob-smacking was the ease with which Ahmed unstrapped the weapon from his shoulder, clicked the safety catch to on and presented the weapon to Fionn.

'No! Strap that over David's shoulder,' Fionn said.

An Arab willingly presenting a loaded gun to an Israeli had to be a first.

'Get away from the back door, Ahmed,' Fionn continued. 'The last thing the boys and girls outside want to see is a friendly Arab face. Sarge, permission to bring David outside?'

The question came as a relief to Sergeant O'Brien because it meant that he could close the gaping jaw that he had only then become aware of. 'Permission granted.'

'Grand. Get the door for us, so. Come on, David, best have a doctor check out Martha's handiwork.'

The head-butter Private Larry marvelled at Fionn's coolness, well, bravery really. All the lads had seen him again and again prove himself by doing strange things, and now Ahmed was calling him the Holy Man. The Holy Man in the Holy City.

The sergeant opened the door and shouted, 'Stand down. We are coming out unarmed.' He didn't expect to be obeyed but at least he got complete silence.

Fionn emerged, back first, leading a neatly bandaged, still armed, Israeli soldier out of the vehicle.

Both men gingerly placed their feet on the ground of the enclosed courtyard. Fionn was now able to gently turn forward and keep David propped up with his arm around his shoulder. He was aware of a semi-circle of some serious-looking weapons pointing at him. What he had in his favour was that the maths was simple. The vehicle passengers were unarmed and David himself was alive and had been reunited with his weapon.

Fionn recognised the captain from the Dead Sea boarding party. They made eye contact and that was the officer's prompt to utter a relieved sentence: 'Out of the vehicle if you please, hands above head.'

The lads joined Fionn and David on the ancient stone slabs, Sergeant O'Brien first and Ahmed last, Peter, Paul, Larry, Michael and Martha in between. Ahmed held his head down, maybe forlornly hoping that his exploits in the van would go unmentioned.

As Pete was passing Fionn, he felt the need to whisper, 'I'd say poor Ahmed is in for it when the Jew lads hear about his shenanigans in the van.'

'How will they hear?' returned Fionn.

'Well, I'm sure David will tell in debriefing.'

'Perhaps not,' was Fionn's simple answer to Pete. 'Perhaps not.'

Martha, who had been listening, spoke to Pete: 'He's gone bleary-eyed ga-ga again.' She didn't seem bothered that she was talking about Fionn within his earshot. 'You know the way he goes, tired-like, zombie-like, when he does his thing.'

'Martha, he only wrapped a few bandages around the lad's eyes.'

'You think?' replied Martha.

'Quiet, and get moving,' the Israeli captain roared.

The eight captives were herded quickly out of the narrow courtyard. They were corralled through ancient labyrinthine passages in what could have passed for being part of the Old City. Maybe it made sense for a modern police depot to use old underground catacomb structures for jails. There were no steps but very much a sense of heading downwards. A not very pleasant smell intensified the further they went, the source of which became apparent when the passageway opened out. It revealed a large semi-circular vaulted cavern completely railed in by a row of floor-to-ceiling prison bars. Sergeant O'Brien estimated there to be about forty inmates behind the bars.

The prisoners were all awake, although many were lying on rough bedding that was strewn about the place. This was a prison and a prison that did not appear to have a toilet, as evidenced by the buckets around the communal cell. The only saving grace to the place was that it had a large, glowing fire in a central position. The fire vented into a hole in the vaulted ceiling. This appeared to be the only source of light and heat in the place.

The Israeli captain continued to be brief in his instructions: 'Back!' This was directed at the, presumably, Palestinian inmates. 'In!' This was directed at the newly arrived group.

Orders are much more reliably followed when they are backed up by ten or so pointing sub-machine guns. It was a hellish place, but if you could ignore the smell, the open blazing fire gave even hell a pleasing aspect.

Ahmed murmured to Sergeant O'Brien as they entered the vaulted cell: 'This is more softening-up tactic, Sergeant. A few hours on your wits dealing with exhaustion and Arab criminals. But these men are not criminal. I will speak for you.'

The barred cell door was closed and the armed guards withdrew. Cameras outside of the bars in opposite corners were clearly keeping an eye on proceedings.

Ahmed gathered an Arab audience around him and started a conversation with a growing number of participants. He stood with his back to the fire, speaking Arabic. The Irish posse was on the other side of the fire, not talking much and not knowing what Ahmed was saying either. They could make out some of it when names were mentioned, and Ahmed would point. Clearly there was some bond between the Jordanian and the Palestinians, or at least they spoke the same language. Ahmed only broke out of his ten-minute discourse to point out to the Irish that the prisoners knew an incident was unfolding above them. The sound of the blast grenade had reached them through their chimney.

At the end of the lecture three of the Palestinians moved around the fire to greet Sergeant O'Brien. They did this by kissing him on both checks, each in turn, and repeating the greeting 'As-salaam alaikum.' The kissing was a source of amusement, or at least light relief for the youngsters. The two Arabs that had already kissed O'Brien moved towards Fionn. They both in turn offered to shake hands but then took the offered hand and bowed low to kiss it, this time repeating 'Al-Quds.' The lads didn't know what the words meant but they could see Fionn's face colouring, mildly embarrassed.

Ahmed spoke: 'These men are political prisoners. Some higher body must think that detaining them in this hell hole will shake the politics out of them. A failed lesson miserably repeated through history.' The three men he was referring to – the greeting party – were leaders and educated men who spoke some English.

'I am Rami from Gaza,' said the shortest of the three. 'Our brother Jordanian tells us of your doings on our behalf and we are most honoured to be soldiers with you. Your acts of bravery will be known to many long before you meet them.'

These kind words were addressed to Fionn, but Sergeant O'Brien felt the need to respond. 'If I was being honest, men, I'd have to say that I'm glad we are all alive at this point. My boys and girl have had more life and near-death experiences in the last eight hours than most Irish soldiers have in a career of service.'

'Regrettably, Sergeant, many of our Palestinian brothers have such experiences daily.' This was spoken by another of the greeters, just marginally the tallest of the men.

It was Sergeant O'Brien who was distinguishing Rami and the rest of the delegation by their physical size. To Irish eyes, he was aware that this big party of men would all look alarmingly similar. Jet black hair, no baldness, all twenty to thirty-five years old, no beards but most with heavy stubble. Good-looking men, at least if they were cleaned up.

The three men, and indeed all the others, focused their gaze on Fionn.

The final member of the trio addressed Fionn directly: 'I am Elias from West Bank near here. We are sorry that your first visit to Jerusalem is to this sorry place. Our Jordanian brother tells us of your holy traits.'

Here we go again, thought Sergeant O'Brien. But he hadn't been in the Glen of Imaal that day. His brain was too fried to rationalise either Ahmed's recovery or Fionn's unexplained appearance in the boat. Maybe that belt in the spine wasn't as severe as it had looked. Maybe the boy was a good swimmer. He was suddenly aware of the two corner cameras outside the cell retraining themselves; presumably there were hidden microphones also listening in on the conversation.

The sergeant was pleased. The Irish usually got on with strangers and the Jews might not have been expecting that. He agreed with Ahmed's view that he and his boys were thrown in there to soften them up before interrogation, but in fact the get-together in a stinking cell was raising everyone's spirits. O'Brien might have learnt a lesson at this point, however: when Fionn was involved, expect the unexpected.

Martha's emotional intelligence was telling her that whatever energy the helping of first Ahmed and then David had sucked out of Fionn, he had not recovered from it yet.

'Thank you, my friend,' said Fionn, 'but the word *holy*, which I am continually hearing, here might be better used to describe a holy show, as my mother would say.'

'I say again, your work against the Jews will be widely known before you meet our free Palestinian people.'

'My friend, Elias, I can only say that I have no work to do against the Jews.'

Rami was keen to speak at this point. 'My friends, we all have work to do against the Jews, and in legion they will be repaid.'

'Not by me, they won't,' said Fionn.

The tallest member of the Palestinian trio, who had not introduced himself when he spoke, broke a little away from Rami and Elias. He had taken on a new role by quietly translating the English and relaying the message to the wider group of Arabs.

'Jaysus, what's he going to say next?' said Pete.

And by God had Fionn something to say. 'Indeed, I have seen heinous acts committed by Jewish men even within the last day. But it cannot be disguised that a savagery has been used against them, as a race, for two thousand or more years. It always struck me' – Fionn paused and then continued speaking a little slower than normal – 'that anti-Semitism is about taking the best of human nature and just using it in reverse. So, you take an industrious and devout community, village, city, country, and you despise and hold these good qualities against them. Maybe simply because you don't see these traits in yourselves. Even that guy Shakespeare got in on the act with his greasy merchant. Hating Jews might have been a pastime throughout the ages.'

The Palestinian translator must have been the best of their English speakers. He was certainly keeping pace in translating Fionn's monologue.

Fionn paused between sentences. An audience would have thought this was for effect. Martha thought that his exertions first with Ahmed, who had christened him the Holy Man, and then with David's afflicted eyes, were the cause.

Even with the pauses Fionn was going to have his say. 'So one day, be you an English crusading king or an insane German dictator, you decide enough is enough. Sure, anyway, didn't they kill the son of God? And all the better if we avenge Jesus' death by looting the better-than-us Jewish civilisation. The hypocrisy of it! Avenging Jesus, the very man who wanted anything but vengeance, blood and viciousness. Crusades me arse, and Third Reich me brown arse. English and German blood-thirsty killing machines, no less. Western civilisation, I ask ye!'

The 'party' was coming to an end before it had even begun. The Irish guys had gathered a little closer together, partly because this was stuff they had never heard Fionn sound off on and because the translator's tone had shifted the mood of the forty-odd Palestinians present. The Irish were getting nervous.

Sergeant O'Brien intervened: 'That's enough for now, Private. We're in enough of a mess here without digging deeper.'

'No, Sarge, I'll have my say. As you say, we're in a mess, and who knows if I'll get to speak my piece again?'

Sergeant O'Brien's mouth just hung open yet again. He thought, only in the Irish Army. Do you think a British Army private would answer back? Not on your life.

Fionn and his translator continued: 'Even here in this unholy of holy cities where there is mayhem and dividing walls, the Jews in the 1960s were humiliated into having the narrowest of access to their venerated Wailing Wall. A pressure keg cemented by the Palestinians and Jordanians together. Of course it was going to blow apart.'

Sergeant O'Brien couldn't help himself: 'Might as well insult the one Jordanian ally we have while you're at it.'

Fionn was in no hurry to reply but he did after a pause. 'The truth is never an insult.'

That was enough. Rami and Elias had by then withdrawn behind their translator. Two and then a third tin cup flew towards the increasingly encircled Irish troop. Larry and Michael readied themselves to deliver a few bruises before they got bruised themselves.

From nowhere a high-powered jet of water doused the fire, sending smoke, steam and hot debris everywhere. Fortuitously, or maybe by design, this created a gap between the newly formed warring factions. The gap was immediately widened when the jet was used to corral the Arabs into the far end of the cell, where they were offered some protection from the spray of water.

The usual eight to ten sub-machine-gun-pointing Israelis were again on hand, this time to extract the seven damp Irish from the cell, with poor Ahmed left to his own devices with his Arab brethren. With the cell door firmly closed again, the now-familiar Israeli captain ushered the troop back through the same labyrinthine passageway they had earlier emerged from.

The captain addressed O'Brien, without stopping him, as he passed.

'Really, Sergeant, you Irish should come with a robust health warning.' The words *health warning* were semi-shouted for effect, as O'Brien had passed five or six paces in front, by then.

The disorientating march led the troop to another cell, this one in a more sanitary condition and in a modern section of the building. It had an open stainless-steel toilet bowl in the corner. No windows and no knowing if they were above or below ground.

Not knowing when they would be called for interrogation and in what order made for a very uncomfortable Friday morning in jail. O'Brien made it clear that all chat among them would be kept general. He felt the cell was certainly bugged and they were to give nothing away that would endanger Sergeant Doyle's troop, wherever they made it to.

Fionn was apparently not finished talking. 'Ahmed will be fine. The Muslims take God a bit more seriously than us Christians. He has faith and thinks God was the instrument of fixing his broken back.'

'How did God manage that? I thought it was you that did the fixing,' said Sergeant O'Brien.

'Maybe, Sarge, both you and Ahmed are right. I did what God directed me to do.'

'Ah here, are you telling us you're being directed by God?' O'Brien asked.

'We're all being directed by God. Jews, Muslims, Christians, the lot. That's probably the only thing we all agree on. I do think God is giving me strength I never knew I had and I'm getting stronger. I was meant to be in Jerusalem.'

No one said anything. Fionn had them spellbound. He'd earned that. Even the most sceptical of observers would have to add up the events, the happenings, and conclude they couldn't all be happenstance, circumstance, coincidence. They had dismissed Fionn's appearance on the detained vessel as an error of perception. Now it was becoming clear that Fionn had appeared on the boat for a reason. A reason that was as yet unclear.

Fionn slept on the floor, oblivious. Martha at one point asked for privacy when the need to use the toilet arose. The lads, on the other hand, didn't give a toss when they wanted to go. They were served one bland rice-based meal at about midday – meagre rations. But Fionn couldn't be roused for it anyway. Even if he could, O'Brien knew he couldn't talk to him about changing boats. There were listening ears.

Chapter **Ten**

Fionn's rest didn't last long.

'You two follow me,' the Israeli captain ordered. He was addressing Sergeant O'Brien and Private O'Toole. 'The rest of you are afforded the dignity of rest before our Sabbath.'

Rest me hole, more likely they were busy collecting intelligence to make the pending interrogations more effective, the sergeant thought. He knew well enough that the Sabbath was from sundown Friday until Saturday evening. There would be no further rest for him and Fionn on the Sabbath, it seemed.

Before leaving, the sergeant gave an instruction: 'Pete, you're in charge.'

'Now we will start with finding out how your small detachment of illegal Irish soldiers seem hell-bent on starting a holy war.'

Disorientated by the comment, O'Brien replied, 'We're not Irish, we're United Nations.'

'You're illegal and you have caused big trouble,' said the captain. 'We like to repay troublemakers in this country.'

The man and the boy were again led down the labyrinth.

Pete had been unlucky in his career. He always

meant to be a good soldier. Somehow things had always got in the way. Being in with the wrong crowd had got him passed over for stripes twice. The army doesn't give third chances. It didn't matter that Pete convinced himself that he would be the exception to the rule. He hadn't been. He felt nearly relieved that Fionn was gone, for the moment. He felt burnt-out and not just from the stresses of the previous night. He had watched Fionn become an emblem that he had originally thought he might keep pace with, stand beside. Pete couldn't dismiss what had happened on that boat with the Israelis: Fionn's appearance from nowhere. Nor could he dismiss the Glen. Even with the highest regard for Fionn, he had to back away. This was about having to admit that you were in the presence of someone extraordinary. While the boys and girl endured their new prison cell, Pete was glad of the respite. The sarge and Fionn were taking the heat from whatever interrogation the Jews were dishing out. His head needed a bit of peace.

'What do you think is going on?' Martha asked.

'I'm guessing they'll be drilling them for info on our boys,' said Michael.

'Lads, you can be as sure as bejaysus we are being listened to. Let's keep that in mind,' Pete reminded them.

'Sure. Sorry, Pete,' said Paul, apologising on behalf of Michael.

'Do you think we'll all be rolled in, Pete?' asked Larry.

'Not you, Lar, anyway. They'd be afraid of your head-butt antics,' replied Pete, still trying to keep the spirits up. There was a bit of a disheartening silence for a moment after Pete's attempt at a joke, so he continued: 'It's still a bit surreal. We're in jail in the most important religious city in the entire world.'

This seemed a bit lost on the youngsters. Their experience of Jerusalem pretty much amounted to incarceration in what for all the world looked and smelt like a medieval dungeon, and now they were in a modern prison cell, complete with one toilet bowl.

'Look, if they call you in, give your name, your rank and state that you're a member of a United Nations official mission. Then keep saying you have nothing else to say,' said Pete.

The excessively large mirror on the back wall was a clichéd giveaway. The emotionless captain ushered the two men into the room where the suited two-man interrogation team were already seated.

'Sergeant O'Brien and Private O'Toole, good afternoon to you. I am Mr X, and may I introduce my colleague, Mr Y. Both of us have been assigned to your case. Because you have committed multiple crimes, it has been a toss-up as to which agency gets you first. Your attempted clandestine landing in our country has drawn much interest from our intelligence agency. On this occasion we trump both the civil and military authorities.'

Mr X was betting the soldiers knew that they were

dealing with Mossad and no names or niceties would be required.

Fionn was having none of it. 'Well, whatever authority you have,' he said, 'I reserve the right not to deal with this X and Y Tarantino bullshit.'

The sergeant intervened: 'That's enough, Private. As a military commander I wish to observe my rights to discuss my unlawful detention with the Israeli military.'

'Perhaps, Sergeant, you should have thought of that before the attempted murder of an Israeli cadet whose father, incidentally, is a senior military officer himself.'

'Nonsense,' responded a somewhat riled Sergeant O'Brien. 'The bloody eejit was tossing what for all we knew was a live grenade into our transporter. And anyway this boy beside me, who you have chosen to pick out separately, expertly tended to the kid. If it was me, I know the tending I would have given him.'

Mr Y, the younger suit, now entered the fray. 'Brave talk indeed, knowing that an Israeli soldier is blinded for life.'

'He could hardly be blinded,' said Fionn.

'Very young to be a medical orderly, are you not?' said Mr X.

It wasn't clear to O'Brien who was the good suit and who the bad. The sergeant felt so wired now that he thought maybe they were both just bad, with a lot more badness behind that glass.

'I meant he was only injured in one eye, and in any

event, I tended to his eye,' said Fionn.

Mr Y seemed a little unnerved. The Irish way of speaking, bastardising the English language, was not to everybody's satisfaction. The words *Jaysus*, *feck* and *eejit* seemed to be thrown in everywhere like verbal grenades.

Mr X stepped in with a change in interviewing tack. 'Your Private Martha O'Dowd's mother is proving to be a most interesting character.'

The knowledge that these men had on O'Brien's troop was thorough, darkly impressive and designed to be disconcerting. What was equally disconcerting to O'Brien was not knowing the fate or whereabouts of Sergeant Doyle and his troop. O'Brien knew he would have to be careful that he or Fionn did not give the Israelis any intelligence that might put their comrades in danger. They must especially keep secret the fact that their planned destination was Bethlehem. If the Israelis went into Bethlehem who knew what would kick off.

'I wouldn't know,' was O'Brien's pissed-off reply. 'Never met the good lady.'

'Well, perhaps you will someday,' Mr Y said, rather menacingly, having regathered himself.

'Mrs O'Dowd finds herself in the media with outrageous claims that this man' – Mr Y pointed at Fionn – 'brought her daughter back to life. Something about unexploded bombs in a training camp. Us Israelis tend not to leave unexploded ordinance lying around. You never know who would pick it up.'

Both Sergeant O'Brien and Sergeant Doyle knew something had happened in Wicklow. Something that had cemented Fionn as the unofficial leader of the group, albeit with Mark as a dissenter. Now was not the time to show his lack of information. The best O'Brien could do was to say, 'We train all our boys to put their comrades before themselves.' A bit lame, he thought.

'Your media has started, since lunch time, reporting the detention of six UN peacekeepers. When last I counted, it was seven,' stated Mr X.

Mr Y took his turn again. 'Indeed, they seem to be of a view that one of your soldiers is missing. I wonder who that could be.'

Mr Y trained his eyes on Fionn.

O'Brien recognised the tactic of further unsettling the interrogatees. But what the sergeant was realising was that he was indeed unsettled. He didn't hold out much hope that the sanctity of life was important to these polished tough nuts. They were menacing, full stop. Building a rapport was not on the agenda. Why were they in such a hurry?

O'Brien wanted to change the direction of the conversation if he could. 'Before ye carry on with any more of your the-world-has-it-in-for-us nonsense, you might do well to remember that this young lad nearly took a beating in that hell hole of a cell for defending the Jewish people.'

'As you have found, Sergeant, from your swift arrest and detention, the Jewish people need very little defending,' said Mr X.

Mr X and Mr Y were operating like a ping ball machine at this stage. When one of them spoke, then it was a given that the other would speak next. O'Brien could only think that referring to yourself by a letter of the alphabet was too clever to be stupid. As the hours elapsed, he became more confident that he and Fionn would give nothing up. A mistake might come through tiredness. However, what really worried him was how the rest of his boys and girl were getting on. On their own they didn't have his experience or Fionn's resilience to rely on. O'Brien's guess was that this interrogation would be halted because one of the other lads had cracked. But he was wrong.

They were endlessly asked the same questions, again and again in different ways. Where were you based in Jordan? For how long? What was the size of your platoon, etc., etc. Bethlehem was not mentioned specifically, but it was clear that the Israeli intelligence was excellent. The very fact that the troop structure *platoon* was repeatedly mentioned said a lot. Six soldiers and a commander was a troop, not a platoon.

By early Saturday morning Mr Y, either by plan or by needing a break from the frustration of getting nowhere, declared, 'Perhaps we have heard enough for the moment.'

Both interrogators stood up as the door behind the sergeant and Fionn opened and a couple of burly armed military police entered to encourage the captives to exit. The sergeant was shoved along the corridor but soon realised the man-handling was to disguise the fact that Fionn had been separated from him. The sergeant was unceremoniously shoved through the corridors and then through the cell door, behind which his five privates were being held. Private Larry responded naturally to seeing his commander roughly handled: he let a fist fly in the direction of the nearest Israeli soldier to the door. He missed. Maybe the Israeli military were becoming wise to the unpredictable Irish.

'Now, Private Fionn, we can perhaps have a more private talk in the absence of your sergeant,' said Mr X. 'Your work since coming close to us has not gone unnoticed. This media rubbish from Ireland does not concern us. You stirring things up in Israel and its neighbouring countries does.'

'I have only helped where I could, only did the job I was sent to do,' replied Fionn.

'Your name is being mentioned on world news channels and we see how you even stirred the Bedouin up in Jordan,' said Mr Y.

'Is there anything worse, for a parent than a sick child? What would I be if I did not do my best to help?' he replied.

'What help were you offering those Palestinian criminals earlier then?' asked Mr X.

'They were misguided in their hatred of all things Jewish and I wanted to explain. The Jews are a chosen people, and what a mess has been made of it all! In the name of God, I ask you.'

These straightforward answers had a cryptic nature

to them, which was frustrating for the interrogators. Their lords and masters were gathered, listening, behind the mirror as the Saturday morning sped on, going nowhere.

Mossad's head of intelligence, Mr Z, had arrived at lunch time on Saturday from Tel Aviv. While in transit he had issued the command for a Knesset member to announce that no Irish soldier was missing. He stipulated that the announcement be made only after a UN statement was issued. The dance was being choreographed. Any mistake was to be put squarely at the Irish Army's door. Therefore, anti-Israeli sentiment about them not searching the Dead Sea for a dead boy would look stupid.

Mr Z took his leave of the room behind the mirror to make a scheduled call to the prime minister. After the call Mr Z, or David as the prime minister addressed him, had Mr X and Y temporarily excuse themselves from the ongoing interrogation.

'The PM has given us till midnight to extract a full story from the prisoner. A failure to do so may, I am told, have fatal consequences.'

'I had perhaps not grasped the gravity of the situation,' the senior Mr X replied.

Mr Y said nothing.

David continued, 'To review, we need answers. Where are his other colleagues? How did he change boats in the Dead Sea? What are his links to the Arab nations? What are his links to the tribal Arabs? The prime minister is clear that this man, this boy, will not be allowed impede us. You have limited time, gentlemen.'

Mr X and Mr Y returned to the interrogation room.

'Tell us Fionn,' said Mr X, adopting a conciliatory tone. 'How many and in what location will we find the rest of your number?'

'Surely with all your technology you should be telling me that. You know, after all, that we made friends with tribesmen in Jordan. Am I to assume that your spy technology let you down?'

Mr Y had regained his voice. 'We are simply looking for confirmation, that is all.'

'Of course, I can confirm that we were attempting to do valuable United Nations work, work which was meant to do no harm and only good. You might say God's work.'

'Well if as you say this is God's work, why are you reticent to answer our simple questions?' asked Mr Y.

'Because, my friend, I suspect you are not interested in my views about God's work. Your great nation has been made great by a common loyalty. Loyalty to the State, loyalty to God. Yet you ask me to be disloyal to my own as if it were a mere nothing. Nothing could ever induce me to do such a thing, not even if torture was involved.'

Mr X thought the misfortune lay in not having enough time for torture.

What disconcerted Mr Y was that Fionn must know what they were thinking. Why else, in God's name, would a prisoner be the person to mention torture?

'Let us ask a different question then,' said Mr Y quickly. 'How and why did you transfer from your original boat?'

'That is of no consequence. I simply must go where I can best serve the mission,' said Fionn.

Mr Z had long since realised that the boy in front of him was not an ordinary young man. Even if torture was an option, he very much doubted if it would work. He equally doubted if Israeli intelligence would countenance allowing the young man his freedom to expand the influence he already possessed.

Chapter **Eleven**

Late Saturday evening, Mr Z – David – discussed the situation with the PM, as arranged.

'Prime Minister, the prisoner Private Fionn is proving to be impenetrable to our most intense questioning. I would request that you sanction the use of more extreme measures.'

'That, my friend, is not an issue, but what is an issue is time. This renegade UN mission even has Trump tweeting. He is at least with us on Jerusalem and I think he likes thwarting the UN's tired old stance that the Holy City is still disputed territory. Why is there a story about a missing soldier in the first instance?' asked the prime minister.

'Our satellite images showed us two boats of similar size close together when we intercepted,' replied Mr Z.

'And why did we not detain both?'

'Our captain is adamant that the searchlights could not have missed the second vessel.'

'Great. With a story that's now capturing world attention, we would appear to be proceeding with a degree of incompetence ourselves.'

'There may be confusion among the Irish as to who was in the vessel we detained,' said Mr Z.

'Good. That might be useful if we need to build on any confusion, especially if there has been bungling going on, on our side,' said the PM. 'You say this private did good work in patching up our young soldier.'

'Yes, Prime Minister, but there is more to it than just that. Our own men are in awe of this boy. He carried out a medical intervention on the Jordanian pilot, injured during our boarding, a medical intervention that could be viewed as miraculous,' said Mr Z.

'Now look, David, this has to be stopped and put to bed before it can grow any bigger.'

'Of course. I'll get on it at once, Prime Minister. There is, however, one more pertinent item to report.'

'Which is?'

'A replay of the satellite footage shows an object move between the two detected vessels.'

'The significance being?'

'We are probing the Irish boy to find out if he was the object transferring between boats. This would explain the confusion about a missing soldier,' said Mr Z.

'Not making any sense, David. Swimming in the Dead Sea?'

'No, sir, the object was moving too fast for a swimmer.'

'Keep concentrating on the private. The sergeant, it would seem, has little more to offer. It's too late to deal with the other detained soldiers. We have all fought hard to build this great nation for seventy years.

What a shame it would be if it all unravelled because of a small thing that we deemed not to warrant our full attention. David, let me assure you this will not happen on my watch. Come back to me with an immediate update if he breaks. One way or another you will receive my final orders. Get that mouthpiece Dannell lined up again to be on the media tomorrow, as a contingency. Just to cover our options, I will extend the interrogation deadline to 6 a.m. Expect my call.'

Chapter **Twelve**

A new low, the lowest, descended at about one o'clock Irish time on Sunday afternoon. The buoyancy that had been created by Knesset member, Dannell, the previous day, was sunk by the same man. He was again in front of the cameras and this time not just Fox.

Dannell was artificially contrite and annoyed at the same time. It apparently wasn't his fault that the Irish Army was mixed up about its troop's strength. 'Six, six – how many times do I have to repeat it? – is the number of legally detained UN warmakers. No, no, no, the Israeli authorities see no necessity for a wild search of the Dead Sea for anyone allegedly missing. If the Irish wanted a search mission, then they should ask their Palestinian and Jordanian friends.'

This breaking news sent the Irish Army command into a tailspin over what it should say next. The despair for Sergeant Doyle and his men in Bethlehem was total. Joe was destroyed. So Fionn was lost after all?

'They must have gotten mixed up and included the pilot of their boat in our number,' said Seamus.

All the hope that had emerged from the Tel Aviv on Saturday was now dead, utterly.

Confusion wasn't the sentiment shared between

Dermot, Mary and Margaret. More like turmoil. When Dermot told Fionn's mother that their joy from yesterday might have been misplaced, both he and Mary were nearly glad that Margaret was too exhausted to take it in. Mary had confided in Dermot that she thought there was a little bit of self-medicating going on. Margaret had access to people who had access to Xanax.

Even the United Nations high command seemed unnerved. A sharp-looking suit on the steps outside New York HQ gave a press statement. The UN were suspending their peacekeeping observation mission and requesting the immediate release of all detained Irish personnel. They looked forward to the repatriation of all thirteen observers in time for Christmas. They, too, were hoping the maths added up, even though the Jordanian captive, Ahmed, didn't get a mention in the press release.

In Bethlehem the Palestinian officials had to suppress their delight at the anti-Israeli PR success of an observer mission that, after all, never got to observe anything except an Israeli jail and Bethlehem hospitality.

Joe was disconsolate but got his comfort and bearings, as he had done all weekend, from his email relationship with Eleanor. He felt he had given Fionn's mother too much hope and Eleanor countered that as best she could.

'Everyone's head is destroyed by how counting the number of boys in custody could be so difficult. Still, don't give up hope,' was her message to try and keep his spirits up.

Monday was a bleak day in early-December Palestine. It was like the world had gone back to work. All the media noise of the weekend in, Dublin, New York, Tel Aviv and Jerusalem was drowned out by sports news.

Sergeant Doyle, in Bethlehem, could tell Irish Army HQ nothing that he hadn't already told them on Saturday. They, similarly, had nothing new to say about when either the Bethlehem-based troops or the Jerusalem captives would be heading home to Ireland. Fionn's fate remained a mystery.

Doyle briefed his men at teatime on Monday evening. He let them know that the Saint Gabrielle would seat them for a private meal and that they were to be in bed by 10 p.m. He would not be joining them to eat. At that stage the whole lot of them were too deflated to be of any use to anyone.

Joe had his head down absently gazing at a keyboard like a man with writer's block.

Fionn rested his hand on Joe's shoulder there in the partial privacy of the hotel alcove. 'My friend, seems like an age,' he said.

Joe turned his head towards the voice, dazed. 'What the feck?' he stuttered as he stood to embrace his buddy, not in disbelief but in total belief at the flesh and blood in front of him.

Taylor and Jake saw the commotion in the alcove from their barstools and came over with what had become the youngsters' chosen greeting: 'My man, Fionn! What the feck?'

It probably would have been *fuck*, but the young soldiers had learnt that the Arabs took a dim view of bad language used only for the sake of using it.

'Que pasa, que pasa?' A half-cut Taylor carried on like he was on a low-budget Spanish holiday.

'Fill us in, fill us in,' said an excited Jake.

'Well, there's lots to tell but very little time to tell it. I know Ireland can be a beautiful and strange little country, but this piece of the world is even stranger and more beautiful,' said Fionn. 'First a bunch of Palestinians wanted to throttle me, and then the Israelis, well, maybe enough said for the moment.'

Joe, who had been emailing soberly, was trying to figure it out. As for Taylor and Jake, their buddy was back, and all was right with the world.

Two days earlier, on Saturday, Joe had shared with his parents the good news that Fionn had been picked up along with the rest of Sergeant O'Brien's troop. He had dared not talk to his old man when on Sunday news emerged from the Israeli spokesman that six had been arrested and not seven. Joe's excuse, in his own head, was that it was impossible to say for sure that Fionn was the seventh soul. Maybe the Israelis were messing with the maths because the Palestinians were scoring kudos over the whole crazy mission. But he knew it was Fionn. And now the relief, for Joe, was immense.

'Boys,' said Fionn, 'you're going to be media

celebrities when ye get home. If the army allow, you might even make it onto *The Late Late*. Ye have to think out what you're going to say.'

'Oh yeah, we'll tell them we are the boys in green, the best you've ever seen and the rest of ye can go shag yourselves,' said Taylor.

'Now listen up,' Fionn said, 'keep the message simple. We do our best and we don't do any harm. We're army, we're Irish and we want the people we serve to do better, try harder, don't hate.'

Joe had gathered himself a bit. 'Good man, Fionn. Sure you'll be there to do the talking, right?'

'No, Joe, my friend, I won't. This is just a fleeting visit. You might say I'm on the run, but I delight in having seen Jerusalem, well a little bit of it anyway. It would be a shame, you might say, not to see a bit more and, well, do no harm. Lads, I have to show you a cruel thing, a thing I honestly prayed you would never have to see.' Fionn unbuttoned the top two buttons of his shirt and revealed something that would be impossible not to recognise, even if you were seeing it for the first time: a bullet-hole wound in the upper sternum.

'Jaysus, that must've hurt,' said Jake.

'It did but that's yet another story for some other time,' said Fionn.

Joe was feeling suddenly unsteady. He got it together and spoke, almost feeling that he was running out of time. 'Are you staying for the meal? What will I tell your ma?'

'Don't worry about my mother. I'll tell her myself.

Jake, I'll have one last glass with the lads before I start making myself scarce. Don't want the natives getting restless.'

Joe's da continued to deal with the emotional roller coaster of that first weekend in a bleak Irish December – deal with it like a bull in a china shop, Mary would have said.

Mary, meanwhile, continued to be the main emotional support for Fionn's mother. The media had decamped from outside Private Martha O'Dowd's house and had re-established themselves outside Private Fionn O'Toole's Glasnevin terraced home. Luckily for his mother, she had long since moved in with Dermot and Mary and the media had yet to track them down.

'Any feckin' media show up here and I'm tellin' ye …' Dermot said without feeling the need to finish the sentence. He couldn't hack that Margaret wasn't following the plot, as he saw it.

That Knesset guy had reappeared in front of the cameras on Sunday, flippantly saying that six captives were in a Jerusalem jail, where according to him they deserved to stay and rot.

'Feckin' failed Rabbi, that fella.' Dermot smelt a rat. The army weren't in touch, and even his own son had gone to ground. He was particularly grumpy on the Tuesday morning because Mary had insisted, for the second day, that he shouldn't go to work while all this was going on. At the breakfast table Dermot was irked by Margaret's continued calmness in the face of her missing son.

Mary thought that Margaret was using a very human coping mechanism. 'Look love, if digging her head in the sand works for her, it's not your place to ram reality down her throat,' she told her husband. Margaret isn't ready for reality yet.'

'I think I'll head home today,' 'Margaret told them as she sat down for breakfast.

'Now don't be hasty, Maggie,' Dermot said. 'Those media hounds are still baying for blood, you know.'

'No, I think they'll be gone,' said Margaret.

'Why so?' asked a calmer Mary.

'Because Fionn told me, or at least he was here,' she replied. 'So I'm guessing all that media kerfuffle is over.'

'What?' said an incredulous Dermot, just about keeping his head.

'Yeah, did you see when ye came down this morning, Mary? I left our two cups in the sink. I didn't want to start rattling the dishwasher around in the middle of the night. We had a cup of tea. He said he'd already eaten.'

Mary and Dermot looked at each other. Mary put her hand on Dermot's knee and squeezed it tightly, a signal that now was not the time for an explosion in his quest to bring order and logic to the world.

Mary calmly asked, 'Where is he now?'

Margaret didn't immediately answer. She was in a reverie now, going over in her mind the reunion with her son.

'Son, I'm not really that surprised to see you. I dreamt you would come. I know you're dead and I know by loving you I must hate the monsters that did this to you. And yes, I already know that's not what you want.'

'Mam, that's the point. We don't die, really. We're all just divine energy. I just have more of it than most poor souls. More in life and more in death. I think I was able to do some good works in life, and I don't see why I shouldn't continue.'

'But, son, where are you? Where is your body?'

Margaret's eyes filled with tears. She felt she couldn't cry for fear of it getting in the way of these precious moments. Deep down she knew something was ending, and no matter how strange, human sadness is a well that cannot run dry.

Mary repeated, 'Where is he now?'

'Oh, gone back. He said his mission wasn't over yet.'

Dermot, with a tightly gripped knee, simply said, 'Maggie, if you do go home today and you do bump into any of those media curs, will ye do me a favour? Don't mention Fionn's visit.'

Epilogue

The president was in imperious mode at the weekly Friday press conference.

'No, I'm not going to condemn the Israeli people for defending their borders, no more than I would condemn the United States for defending its borders with Mexico. If the United Nations wants to send Irish military on half-baked errands then, you know what, there are consequences. No, the United States won't be intervening in the dispute. Soldiers go missing. That's just the way it is.

'Don't you just get a bit tired of this fake news from the Irish? You know, I'm going to tell you, if these leprechaun shenanigans are kept up, I'm not so sure we can do the Saint Patrick's Day thing in the White House going forward.'

A reporter from NBC asked, 'Are you aware, Mr President, that Palestinian women are being denied entry into Jerusalem when they state that the purpose of their visit is to seek the Messiah?'

'I just think,' said the president, 'if you're looking for a Messiah, then Jerusalem is a very good place to start, right?'

Printed in Great Britain
by Amazon

52429076R00088